CLOSING THE CIRCLE

P A WILSON

FREE EBOOK

Claim your copy of Buying Into Death when you sign up for my newsletter and follow Charity as she solves her fastest case yet!

ONE

The body lay in the parking lot of the Palace of Fine Arts. The circle and five-pointed star carved on his chest illuminated blue then red in the flashing lights of the two patrol cars parked at the edge of the grass.

San Francisco fog crept from the shadows and curled around the corners of the buildings. The columns leaned over the group of people as though listening. Four people stood talking in the pool of light. Two of them wore uniforms, two suits.

Sam Barton took his FBI ID folder from his jacket pocket as he walked toward the sound of voices, voices that burst in short rhythms. The cadence of questions, not conversations. The phone call that dragged him into the pre-dawn fog cut short the hope that he had left the brutal world of serial killers behind him. They said they needed someone who knew about rituals, and they didn't care that he came to San Francisco to get away.

Sam walked toward the grass in front of the Exploratorium. He saw one of the suits, a tall solidly built man gesture to the uniformed woman. The big detective's partner, shorter but broader, said something then walked toward the body.

"Who called it in?" Sam heard the taller detective ask.

"A woman jogging by," the uniformed woman answered. "I have no idea what she was doing out at this time. All by herself, for Christ sake."

"You do what you have to, I guess," the shorter detective called back over his shoulder. "Any ID on the body?"

"Good morning detectives," Sam said before the woman could answer.

"Who the hell are you?" The taller detective asked, putting his hand on his gun.

Sam flipped open his ID holder, experience told him that it was better to have his credentials ready. "Special Agent Sam Barton. I got a call that you might need me."

"Morton," the detective answered and pointed to his partner. "This is Kang. Who called you?"

"My section chief." Sam looked at the uniformed woman. "You were the first on the scene?"

"Yes." She looked at Morton and when he did not make the introductions, she said, "Dickson." holding out her hand to shake Sam's. "My partner here is Kelly."

"Great, now that the social niceties are done," Morton snapped. "Why did they call you in?"

"It looks like your partner has found something," Sam spoke to officer Dickson, not biting on the aggression from Detective Morton. "What have you got there?"

Officer Kelly walked over to them, a business card held in his gloved fingertips. He looked at Detective Morton, then stopped and waited.

The cop stepped between Sam and Kelly. "I'm the detective on site. Until that changes, I'll take charge."

Sam chose not to argue. He was used to the local cops acting like dogs pissing to mark their territory.

"Business card," Kelly said as he handed it to Morton. The

detective pulled an evidence bag out of his pocket. "It was on the grass. It's for a Felicity Armstrong. Business called Help On Demand."

Detective Kang looked at the body. "That's not a woman. Let's hope Ms. Armstrong is alive and helpful."

Sam walked to the body. He sensed Morton step just behind him, still protecting what he thought was his territory.

"This is why they called me." Sam pointed to the naked dead man.

"Yeah. I figured it wasn't just because some guy got killed in the night." Morton looked down at the chest of the victim. The circle was cut deep into the flesh, the points of the star piercing the edge.

Sam rubbed his hand through his wavy, dark brown hair. This was going to be a bad day.

FELICITY ARMSTRONG HEARD voices in the small lobby of Help On Demand. She stepped out of her office to join the three people chatting at a desk.

"I think I'm going to be the final bidder on the tickets. This is my last chance. Man, U2 in Hawaii at Christmas." Isaac sighed.

Felicity grinned at his enthusiasm. At twenty-eight, he still got enjoyment from teenage activities like concerts. Since she lost her family, she had found friendships with her staff, Isaac was more a little brother than an employee.

"Isaac, that's great. I wish I could have my Christmas plans made by September," Felicity said. "Will you need time off?"

"Yes. Well, I was going to talk to you about that." Isaac gave her a huge grin. "I'm going to try to get a flight late on Friday night and then come home on Sunday, but I might need to leave early on Friday."

"Okay, let me know as soon as possible." She waited but Isaac didn't respond. "We'll figure something out with the schedule."

"Yes, boss." Isaac gave her his sweet and innocent smile.

"Okay," Felicity said. "I guess we should get back to work. Me included."

"Yes, oh high and exalted mistress," Isaac sighed and gave a dramatic roll of his eyes. "Ryan and Amanda were going to do the filing. Why don't we go over the job list for next week?"

"Sure, let's do that. It's better than paperwork," Felicity said. She pushed her auburn curls back behind her ears and led Isaac into her office.

A half hour later, Felicity and Isaac were finished making the list of staff to call for the assignments. They heard feet banging up the stairs. "Wow. They aren't afraid to let us know they're coming," Isaac said, getting up to greet whoever was about to come in the door.

Felicity listened to the conversation as she cleared the mess of paper on her desk.

"Is Felicity Armstrong here?" By the strong authority to the voice, the man was not looking for a job. Or if he was, his attitude needed adjusting.

"May I ask who would like to see her?" Isaac carefully did not answer the specific question. Felicity wondered why he was being so coy.

"Yes, you may," the voice answered. "Detectives Morton and Kang, SFPD."

"Okay," Isaac said. "Yes, she's here." He pressed the intercom and called her to the front.

"What can I do for you, Detectives?" Felicity glanced at the identification they still held out.

"Is there somewhere we can speak in private?" Detective

Morton looked at Isaac who was sitting forward in his chair, obviously all ears.

She pointed to the open door of her office, and the two detectives motioned for her to go ahead of them. As soon as the door closed, Detective Morton leaned against it.

"Have a seat," Detective Kang said placing a large white envelope on her desk.

Felicity sat in her chair. Her eyes seemed to be stuck on the envelope. Coldness filled her stomach.

"I would like you to look at some pictures and tell me if you recognize the man in them."

The pictures were large, black and white matte finished. The lighting used in the photography made the details sharp and lifeless. A man's face, eyes closed, filled the center of the photo.

"Lord and Lady," she whispered. "He looks dead."

"Yes." Detective Morton moved away from the door and punched his finger into the center of the picture. "Dead people tend to look that way. Do you know him?"

Felicity took a deep breath and looked closely at the picture. She wanted to be sure of her answer. The man's stillness made it difficult for her to imagine him in life. She tried to imagine the face showing laughter, or anger, some emotion that would trigger a memory. All she saw was absence.

"I'm sorry," she said, pushing the photo toward the detectives. "I haven't seen a body before, so I don't really know how different people look when they're dead. I'm pretty sure I don't know him, though."

The two detectives looked at each other and then turned back to her.

"We found your business card near the body," Detective Kang said. Felicity realized they were trying to keep her on edge by snapping sentences at her. The realization did not do anything to reduce their success. "Are you sure he's not a client."

She picked up the pictures again, two different angles of the same subject. "I can't be totally sure. I don't meet all my clients. I can tell you it's not one of my temps, though."

"Do you know all your temps?" Morton pulled the pictures out of her hand.

"Yes," she said, keeping firm control over her rising anger. "I meet everyone I hire. We are fairly small, so I still know all the employees. Clients are different. I have a lot of clients. They give out my business cards because they like my service. That means I don't know everyone who has my card in their pocket."

Morton slid the pictures back in the envelope. "Okay, thank you for your time."

"There's one more thing before we go," detective Kang said. "Where were you last night?"

She realized that they thought she was connected to the murder. "I worked here until about eight. I walked home. On the way, I stopped to get take-out sushi. I got home just before nine, ate dinner, watched television, and went to bed."

Morton made notes in a small notebook. "Can anyone confirm this?"

"They might remember me at the restaurant. It's called Sushimi." Morton made another note, then seemed to wait for more. "My downstairs neighbor was going out as I got home. I think that's it."

"Your address, please."

"Am I a suspect? Should I be contacting a lawyer?"

"You are not a suspect," detective Morton said. "We'll check with your neighbor and the restaurant, but you probably don't need to worry about a lawyer."

"Probably?" Felicity knew the police could lie about her

being a suspect and this seemed too easy. "Why don't I need to worry?"

"You aren't a suspect, which should be enough," Morton said.

Felicity gave them her address and tried not to think about what the pictures hid. "Do you have any idea who he might be?"

"No," detective Morton answered, snapping the notebook closed and looking up at Felicity. "If we need anything, we'll be in touch. You aren't planning any trips outside the city, are you?"

Felicity shook her head. "You can find me here most of the time."

TWO

Mick pushed the shopping cart through union square. He hunched over the handle of the cart, the layers of worn clothing he wore blurring the shape of his body into a black bulky lump. Under sheets of newspaper and rags, other anonymous piles of clothing slept on benches.

The front left wheel of his cart squeaked and twisted. Mick tugged slightly pulling it back into line. It was 3 am and he had to find an empty bench, or he would be sleeping in a doorway again. That did not work as well for him. He hated being woken up by a shopkeeper or office worker yelling at him. In the park, the cops just came by and tapped you on the foot to move you along. They only got nasty with guys who did not move on politely.

Mick stopped the cart and pulled up the red scarf he had found on a bench at Fishermen's Wharf earlier today, yesterday really. You need to filter the dampness of a San Francisco fall night through something, or else it cooled you too much. Keeping warm was critical to surviving the streets.

"Lord, I appreciate you are trying to teach me a lesson, but I sure would like a bit of warmth now," he shouted to the sky.

A chorus of groans and shouts came from the benches in protest of the broken peace.

"Sorry," he shouted to them, "the Lord don't hear so well."

It was difficult for him to see clearly through the small gap between the greasy back hoodie and the torn scarf. He could just make out which benches were empty, but nothing else unless he bent his neck to change the line of sight. When he bumped into something on the ground it surprised him, the paths were usually clear. Anything worthwhile was scavenged, everything else kicked away.

The something was hard but yielding. Mick could not push through it or roll over it.

"God, now what have you put in my path to test me?" His voice held to a mumble, so he did not disturb the sleepers again.

Moving around to the front of his cart, Mick saw what was there. It was a woman - or it used to be a woman. Mick looked at the markings on her naked body and the world seemed to fade from the edge of his sight. No matter how badly he wanted to, he knew he could not just leave her there.

"God, for crying out loud, it's okay to test *me* with the devil's work, but kids come here. What are you thinking?" He sighed and looked around. Everyone else was asleep, or pretending to be, so they would not get dragged into it. At this time in the morning it was wise to be invisible.

Mick knew he needed to find someone to deal with this, and probably report it to the police. It was going to be a bitch getting someone to pay attention. The lights from the lobby of the St Francis were the closest. He'd walked past the same guy at the door for the last six months, it was the closest to a relationship he came these days. Pushing his cart around the body on the walkway, Mick made his way across Powell Street to talk to the doorman.

. . .

FELICITY SAT in her office listening to bland on-hold music. She was holding for Anson Weathers, a long-term client.

"Hi, Felicity," Anson's voice was a pleasant change from the country music she had been trying to ignore.

"Hi, I know you're busy right now, so I'll get to the point. Do you have any idea when you are going to need Amanda next?"

"Yes, three days next week if she's available. There's a trade show I need to attend, and she can help with the booth."

"I'll have her call you so you can work out the details." Felicity made a note then reached for the list of numbers to call, ready to close the conversation.

"Thanks." Anson paused. "Hey, did you hear about the body they found?"

"No." Felicity thought of the pictures the police had shown her, but she'd not heard anything on the news. The thought of discussing it with Anson brought back the chill she felt looking at the dead man. She started to tell him she needed to leave for a meeting when he began the story.

"I have a friend who works at the St Francis. Some homeless guy came over and told him about a woman he found in the park. My buddy is pissed he can't sell his story to the papers. The cops told him they'd run him in if he did."

"Did you say a woman?" Felicity hoped she'd heard wrong. The list of calls sat ignored on her desk.

"Yes, some woman in the middle of Union Square – last night. Well early this morning, really."

Two bodies. Felicity shivered. What was going on? The city was not really a place where big crimes like this happened on a regular basis. Lots of petty theft, but not murder, at least not until lately. "Do they know who she is?" she felt compelled to ask.

"My buddy had no details beyond the fact that the body was a mess. He didn't get to see it. Sorry, that sounds bad. He just called the cops, and they told him and the homeless guy to wait at the hotel. The homeless guy wasn't much help. He just kept saying God was testing him."

"I hope they find out who she is soon. And catch the killer, of course. I feel for the family, someone is in for really bad news." She tried to ignore the shiver that crossed her shoulders.

"I guess you're right." Anson sighed. "Listen, I have to go. Take care."

Closing the call with Anson, Felicity sent a quick prayer to the Lord and Lady that this would be the end of the killings. "Give the police the help they need to find this person."

THREE

Every morning at five, Malcolm Kingston, retired accountant, took his bearded collie for a walk along Jefferson Street and up the grass beside the cable car station toward Hyde and Beach. Some days it was the only exercise they got.

This morning it was raining and Alfie, his dog, looked more like a giant rat than his usual fluffy sheepdogish self. The rain was heavy enough that Malcolm could not see much beyond the few feet in front of them. As usual, when Alfie sensed the end of the walk, and his end of walk treat, he pulled harder on the leash. On autopilot, Malcolm almost slipped and fell when Alfie pulled to the right rather than continuing up Hyde Street.

"Alfie, stop." He used the voice that was supposed to make him the alpha dog. It didn't work, Alfie just kept pulling.

"Okay, you win." Malcolm sighed, knowing his life would be easier if he let the dog have its own way. Walking over to where Alfie stood, tail wagging, Malcolm allowed the lead to retract into the handle. Alfie was snuffling at a large shape.

"Sit!" Malcolm pulled on the leash and Alfie abruptly obeyed the command.

"Oh, dear, are you okay?" Malcolm addressed the woman

who seemed to have passed out face down in the shrubs at the foot of the hill. A tee shirt dress clung to her body. When she made no response, he reached out to turn her over. When he pulled at the dress, it came away in his hand. The woman was dead and naked.

Malcolm pulled out his cell phone and dialed 911, pushing away the nausea that flowed through him. His voice shaky, he had to repeat himself several times before the woman on the line understood. "I said there's a dead woman behind the cable car station, on Hyde just uphill from Jefferson. The bushes, yes, the ones right at the bottom of the station. You need to send the police. No, I can't see anyone else around. Yes, I'll wait, but please hurry."

He pulled Alfie away from the body and sat on the concrete just within sight of the woman. He had to keep fighting his urge to cover her with his coat. The police would not want him doing anything more to disturb the scene. He knew that from television detective shows. Malcolm kept looking at the cuts in her back. Even though it increased his nausea, it was impossible not to look. There were stars and curved lines slashed into the flesh.

WHEN THE POLICE ARRIVED, they worked efficiently, gathering information, calling for experts, and reassuring Malcolm.

Officer Kelly turned from the body and looked at Malcolm, seeing a tall bald man on the far side of sixty. He made note of Malcolm's contact information.

"Thank you, Mr. Kingston. Just sit here in the car until the detectives come. You won't get any wetter in there." Malcolm seemed happy to comply. He probably knew he would have to answer questions and smiled briefly as though to say he would do what needed to be done.

"Walt, come over here," his partner's voice came out of the darkness. The rain was keeping the night around longer than normal.

"On my way." Walt closed his notebook and nodded to Malcolm before turning away.

"What's up, Eve?" Officer Kelly walked toward the pool of light that marked his partner's position. She was shining her flashlight into the shrubs, a few feet along the footpath on the other side of the body.

"Keep quiet. We don't want him to know we've found this. If he's involved, well," she lifted the flashlight a foot farther into the bush, "we might have a problem."

In the pool of light, Kelly saw an arm, it was bloated and misshapen, but it was definitely an arm. As Eve shifted the beam of the flashlight higher, he could see the rest of the body.

He looked over his shoulder to see the old man bent over, patting his dog. He looked too meek to have done this, but you never know.

"No shit, we have a problem. I'll call it in. You want to go back to the car and make sure Mr. Kingston stays put?"

FOUR

Felicity stood in her galley kitchen sipping black coffee from a "world's greatest boss" mug. She looked out through the pass-through to the street beyond. The fog had burned off. It looked like the day was going to be sunny and warm again. There would only be few more nice days before winter settled. San Francisco winters tended toward wet and chilly. She thought that was a blessing when she considered the effect that snow and steep hills could have on traffic.

Early commuters were hurrying to the bus or cable car stops. As she watched, a few cars went by, but San Francisco was not a car friendly town – too many hills, too many tourists – most people Felicity knew walked or bussed to work.

The radio playing in the background finished the weather report, and the music introducing the news broke into Felicity's daydream. She put the mug on the counter and checked her face in the mirror. Auburn curls tied back, minimal makeup, and her pale green suit, complemented her pale complexion. She noticed the new tension lines on her forehead and smoothed them gently. The radio changed from music to the news, her cue to get ready to leave so she could be at the office before her day got too busy.

... two bodies were found in the last two days and two more today in the area of the Hyde Street Cable Car stop. The police have no comment, but we have information from a confidential source that the last two bodies were found this morning around five thirty. We have information that there was a ritualistic aspect to the deaths and the police have formed a belief that we have a serial killer in the city.

Dropping her purse back on the counter, Felicity put a shaking hand on her stomach and took a deep breath. Two more deaths. Lord and Lady, what was going on? She decided that being early for work was less important than praying for protection. Pulling a wooden box from the cupboard above the fridge, she carried it to the living room. After placing the box on the side table, she pulled aside the rug from the floor in front of the fireplace. Underneath was a circle painted in white on the wooden floorboards.

She slipped out of her low heels, took a red candle and a lighter from the box, and stepped into the circle. Standing in the middle, Felicity placed the candle facing the fireplace. She took another deep breath to center her thoughts before speaking. "I call the Spirit of the East, air, to join with me in this prayer."

She moved a quarter turn counterclockwise.

"I call the Spirit of the North, earth, to join us in this prayer."

Another turn, "I call the Spirit of the West, water, to join us in this prayer."

Turn, "I call the Spirit of the South, fire, to join us in this prayer."

Turning to face the east again, she sat in the center of the warded circle.

After lighting the candle, Felicity clasped her hands loosely in her lap and breathed deeply four times. "I call to you Lady, as protection and wisdom, to look on this city and change the darkness that has fallen upon us." Felicity waited calmly for the feeling that always came to her when she practiced the rituals of her religion. The warmth that filled her was as comforting and reassuring as her mother's love. It came today quickly as though the Lady had been waiting for her call.

"I thank you, Lady, for your presence. I ask your protection for the people of the city as this darkness passes, as all things must. I ask you to give clarity to the police so they can find the person who is committing these crimes. I thank you for your presence today."

Breathing deeply again, Felicity raised her arms up and around in a circle bringing the palms together and dropping her hands in her lap. She stood again and faced the fireplace. "Spirit of air, East, I thank you and release you from the circle." Turning clockwise this time, she moved around the circle releasing the spirits from their guardian roles.

Felicity faced east again and sat in the center to blow out the candle. She sat quietly for a few minutes to allow the spirits time to clear the circle, and for her mind to refocus on the outside world. Standing, she stepped out of the circle, placed the candle back in the box, and rolled the rug back into place.

WHEN SHE ARRIVED at work an hour later, Felicity interrupted her staff in mid-gossip.

"I've heard everything from 'it's a Satanist ritual sacrifice', to the 'deaths aren't related it's just the press selling papers'," Isaac said, glancing at Felicity to draw her into the conversation. "What have you heard?"

"You know what? I'm already tired of hearing about these murders. It seems that now the news has come out, the press is indulging in the usual frenzied activity of developing suppositions to fill the void." Felicity grabbed a coffee and started for her office. "Can we just pretend it's not happening, at least for a couple of hours?"

"Spoil sport." Isaac pouted. "I guess it can't hurt to let the rumors develop unaided until this afternoon."

"I'm sorry to be such a wet blanket, but let's try to remember that it's not a reality show. There are four families mourning loved ones." Her shoulders shivered with fear and tension.

"No. I'm sorry, you're right. Anyway, I was telling these guys, I won the tickets and I've booked my flight to Hawaii. It's all ready to go, I just need hotels now."

Felicity smiled at his enthusiasm. "That's great news. Good luck on the hotels, Christmas in Hawaii might be a bit of a challenge."

"Well, you know me, if there is a way I will find it." Isaac pulled open a drawer. "I'll update some of our recruitment ads, the pool of temps is getting a bit low, and we don't want to run out of people who can fill the slots."

Felicity picked up the pile of FAX requests for temporary help, happy to see business coming in at about the same volume as last week. Isaac had sorted them by skills required and notice time. He might be a gossip, but he was also a great assistant.

In her office, she booted up her computer and opened the skills inventory, ready to match names to requirements. By the time lunch hour arrived, she had completed the inventory and called six people to check availability. The sound of voices at the front desk drew her attention away from the work.

"Ms. Armstrong is tied up right now." Isaac's voice carried that flirty sound. Felicity felt her curiosity rise. Isaac was usually very professional with clients.

"Oh, well, I guess that lets you interrupt a lot of business. If you ever want to get my attention, you just have to ask." Felicity could only hear a low growl of answers to Isaac's comments. "Wait here and I'll get her."

Her curiosity sent her to the lobby to see for herself who was making Isaac flirt so outrageously. Putting on her confident business face, Felicity stepped out and looked up into the slate grey eyes of a tall man standing across the desk from Isaac. She understood why Isaac was flirting. The man stood just the right amount over six feet, dark wavy hair and slate grey eyes added to the picture, and nicely built seemed to be a phrase designed for him. She realized her eyes were wandering down his body but could not stop herself. When her gaze dropped from his broad shoulders, she noticed his outstretched hand. In it he held official looking identification with FBI printed behind a shield.

"Hi, I'm Felicity Armstrong." She heard the breathiness in her voice and silently told her hormones to grow up. "You wanted to see me?"

"Can we go somewhere private?" He put his ID back in his pocket.

"Certainly. May I have a closer look at your identification?" She pulled herself together and drove the hormones back where they belonged.

"Name's Sam Barton." He pulled it out again and handed it to her. The words, Special Agent Barton, Samuel were printed on the card. "I have a few questions for you."

Showing Sam into the office, Felicity threw a quelling glance at Isaac, who was miming behind Sam's back, making kissing gestures. She pointed Sam to the chair usually used by job candidates. Sitting in her own chair, she waited for him to start asking questions. She assumed he was here about the murders, there was no other reason the FBI would come to her. All the same, she was in no hurry to get to the subject and was happy to enjoy the view.

Sam remained standing, pulling out a notebook, and reading

his notes for a few pages, flipping the sheets without looking up. Finally finished with the review, he looked at her and frowned. "I assume you've heard the news this morning."

"Yes, the reporter said you think there is a serial killer here."

"They make up information to fill the blanks. We have no official status to report."

"Are you saying that the bodies were not marked?"

"I'm saying there's no official serial killer case." He shifted his pose slightly, and Felicity felt the authority of the FBI fill the room. "Ms. Armstrong, you know that your business card was found with the first body."

"I understand it was found near the site, yes."

"And you claim not to know the victim."

"You make that sound like I'm lying. I don't just claim that I don't know him, I really don't." Tension gripped her body, anger rising from her stomach, muscles tightening. She felt her posture change with the reaction. Instead of being intimidated, as she was sure he intended, she felt imperial as though he was not allowed to sit in her presence. Felicity knew the danger of following those feelings and knew that she needed to be careful not to allow them to push her into a shouting match.

"Yes, so you told the police." Sam leaned against the wall, his relaxation matching her rising tension.

"Yes." Felicity offered nothing else.

He looked down at his notebook. "Do you know an Agnes Thomas?"

"No, I don't." She swallowed acid building in her stomach.

"You answered fast. Are you sure? You said you have a lot of clients. She was in her mid-fifties."

"I can check my files, but I have few female clients, and I know I don't have a staff member by that name. Did she have my card on her?"

"Lila Rose? She was fifty-one, tall."

"Did I know her?" Felicity heard her voice tighten and took a calming breath. "No, no client named Lila Rose, no staff member. What makes you think I know her?"

"David Adams, he was..."

The anger turned to nausea, cold sliding down her body. "He is my friend."

"I'm sorry. He was the fourth victim."

"No. It must be another David Adams, it's a common name." Felicity reached for the phone and dialed David's cell phone. "He always answers his mobile. It must be a mistake. Someone else, or maybe someone stole his identification."

She held the phone to her ear until the call connected to voice mail. Sam reached across the desk, took the handset from her, and hung it up. "He was identified by his sister, Janice Bryant. We called her based on the emergency number in his phone. There's no mistake. He's been dead about a week, but she was able to identify him by the tattoos on his shoulder. And she told us he was your friend."

She stared at the desktop in front of her, how could David be the victim of such a crime, he was gentle and kind. How did he come into contact with someone who could murder people?

"I guess that explains why you're here. Did she send you to me? Can you tell me how it happened? Is she still in town? I should be with her." If she could get some details, she might be able to understand why this happened. She needed to help David's soul on its journey to the Summerlands. Before she could do that, she must help herself and find some peace, or at least understanding.

Beeping came from his pocket. He pulled out a BlackBerry and checked the screen. "I'm sorry I have to go. You aren't planning any trips in the next few days, are you?"

"Am I a suspect?" Fear replaced the nausea. Her day had steadily darkened since the radio announcement this morning.

"No. Not yet." He turned to go. "I will need to ask you more questions, though." He shut the door and Felicity was left alone with her grief and fear for a long minute until Isaac put his head inside.

"Are you coming out to dish the dirt sweetie?" He looked into her face and his tone changed. "Oh, honey, what's wrong?" He moved to her side and gave her a hug. "It's okay, everything will be fine."

Felicity had a hunch it would not be fine, at least not for a very long time.

FIVE

After Isaac and Amanda left for the day, Felicity decided to get a start on the stack of files that had been sitting on her desk for a week. Then the thought of going home gave her a chill, the office felt less lonely than her home would. Here echoes of the daily activity filled the empty spaces.

The take-out box on her desk was empty, but Felicity could still smell the black bean sauce. Normally her favorite aroma, today, after all the bad news and stress, it just made her feel sick. Pain was building at her temples, and now she wanted to get home before it developed into a full-blown migraine.

She carried the take-out box into the kitchen and dropped it in the garbage. Stretching her neck and shoulders to loosen up the tension that had been building for the last three hours, she decided it was time to go home. The cleaners would be arriving soon, and she hated to be there while they worked. Realizing she needed to burn some stress and adrenaline from her system, Felicity decided to walk. She grabbed a bottle of water from the fridge before heading back to her office.

She heard footsteps on the stairs leading to her floor. "Damn." She hadn't locked the door behind Isaac, and those footsteps did not belong to the cleaners. "Idiot, leaving the office unlocked is not a good idea these days." She hurried to turn the catch on the door and made it just before the footsteps arrived at the top of the landing.

When the person tried the doorknob instead of knocking, she felt relieved that she won the race. Who tried a door to a business at nine on a weeknight? When turning the handle did not produce the expected result, the person on the other side knocked, hard and angry.

"Ms. Armstrong, are you there?"

Felicity's fear blocked her ability to think. The voice was familiar, but she could not concentrate on identifying it through the sudden wave of fear overwhelming her. "Ms. Armstrong, it's Sam Barton."

Relief left her almost as dizzy as the fear. "Just a second."

As she unlocked the door, Sam turned the handle again and Felicity stepped back. "What took you so long to get to the door?" He was reaching for the gun she could see in the holster under his jacket. "Is something wrong?"

"No. Calm down." Felicity waved her hands to calm him. She wondered at his strong reaction, had something changed? Was there another body? "I just didn't want to leave the door open, and I worried about who was coming up the stairs. I'm fine."

"You know it's dangerous right now to be working late alone." He seemed to relax as he locked the door. "Until we know why these people are being killed, we don't know who's in danger."

"Well, I appreciate you being worried, but weren't all the victims middle-aged?" Felicity was surprised to find she was relieved that someone was worried about her. Sam's protective-ness felt comforting.

"Yes, but we're not sure what facts form the pattern. Their

ages might be coincidence. The fact that two of them are connected to you could be nothing but coincidence too."

"Why are you so concerned about me? There are lots of potential victims outside this building." Felicity felt a shiver cross her shoulders.

"Yes, but as far as we know at this point, only you and the killer have connections to more than one of them."

"So, am I a potential victim or a suspect?" Felicity did not like where this conversation was going. Her nerves were stretched tight, and she could feel her head start to throb again. It would not take much to push her into tears or fury. She took a calming breath and pushed her anger down. Later tonight, she would meditate, and ask the Lady for balance and calm. Now, she just needed to make sure she did not get into more trouble. She needed to get through the next few minutes without breaking down. Tears would not help anything.

"Well, good question." Sam sat in one of the chairs at Isaac's desk. "Right now, you are either a very clever and twisted murderer, or you are a potential victim. We need more data."

"I hope you get it soon." She realized as she spoke how that would happen. "I hope it won't take any more deaths to get you what you need to know. Now, do you have questions for me, or are you here for something else?"

"I have some more questions." Sam pulled out his notebook. "Agnes Thomas, victim number two, frequented the Roxy movie theatre. It's a block from here. Have you ever been there?"

"Yes, we all went there for a lunch movie treat." Felicity rubbed her temples trying to relax the pain building there.

"Did anything unusual happen?" He kept his eyes directly on her face.

"I don't remember anything. Do you think I ran into her?"

She realized the headache was not going to fade without medication.

"Maybe." He flipped a page in the notebook.

"Look, I'm really tired, is there anything else?" Felicity opened her desk drawer, looking for aspirin.

"Yes."

"Could we please do this another time?" She could hear the strain in her voice.

"No. I only have a few more questions," Sam said. He looked up from his notebook. "Are you okay? You look like you are going to keel over."

"I was on my way home when I heard you coming up the stairs. I have a blinding headache, and I need time to absorb what has happened to my friend. I need to go home." She felt the pressure of tears in her throat and eyes. Felicity knew she would not be able to remain in control much longer. She needed to get home.

"Okay, let's hope there isn't another victim tonight." He put his notebook in his pocket.

"What's that supposed to mean?" Finally losing control, she stood and put her hands on her hips. "I'm happy to help, but I don't have any control over what this person is doing. I may have some connection to two of the victims, but the last one was my friend."

"I didn't mean anything by it. You're right, the murderer is in control right now. Until we have more information, we can't do anything. You aren't the only one who is hoping that it doesn't come in the form of another death."

"Okay." She ran her hands through her hair and reminded herself that Sam was trying to solve some ugly murders. "Look, come back tomorrow morning around nine, and I'll be in better shape to think. I just need some sleep."

"How are you getting home?" Sam stepped toward her taking her elbow.

"I was going to walk, but now I'm going to call a cab. I don't think I'll have the energy, or nerve, to do anything else." She moved out of his reach.

"I'll drive you." He appeared to be waiting for her to get her things.

"No need. I'd be more comfortable taking a cab." She did not want to spend time chatting on the short drive. Nor did she want to give him directions to her place. She just wanted to tell the cab where to go and sit back until she was home.

"Not a problem. I would feel more comfortable knowing you got home. It's not a long ride and you don't have to answer questions, I swear." Was he reading her mind? "I know your address, it's in your file, so you just need to get your things, and lock the door behind us."

SIX

Wilma Jones looked around while her partner turned the cruiser into the parking lot at Telegraph Hill. The Coit Tower rose into the predawn sky. She smiled at the thought of all the tourists who commented on its suggestive shape. She knew the tower was designed as a fluted column and was a gift from Lillie Coit to beautify the city. Wilma figured that building a giant penis on a hill was an interesting way to do that.

As soon as Jules stopped the car, they got out, turning on their flashlights. If they didn't move some of the street people early, the guides on the first tour buses would raise hell. The homeless sometimes slept in the parking spaces, using their carts to cut the wind, and a couple of times a bus almost ran over someone.

"Okay," Jules said, pointing to the far side of the lot. "Let's start there."

"Fine, let me get the bags." Wilma pulled two grocery bags from the back of the car.

"You know they call you the 'social worker' back at the station." Jules pointed to the bags. "Why do you bother?"

"I hate that we have to move these people along. They need

to sleep somewhere." She hung both bags from her left hand and flashed the light around the circle. "It doesn't cost me much, and at least they get a sandwich and a juice box a day."

Jules shrugged. "Okay, fine. I'll keep my eyes open, and you do the good work."

"Oh yeah, like there's been a problem up here in years." Wilma shook her head. A damp wind slid around the cruiser and chilled her exposed face. They circled the statue and started waking sleepers. Jules walked with his right hand on his gun.

The doorway and entry steps were free of sleepers. Wilma's flashlight showed no piles of clothes or plastic bags, the usual bedding for overnighters. There were a few sleepers under the trees, one or two snuggled up to the wall around the statue of Christopher Columbus. She could see a couple of shopping carts in the far corner of the lot.

"Wake up." Wilma prodded a lump of clothes curled in the shadow of a tree, inside a circle of dripping condensation. "Is that you, Marty?"

The man under the pile of coats and sweaters mumbled something as he rolled over.

"Here, have something to eat." She held out a sandwich. "Are you moving?"

"Leave me be woman." Marty's breath was forty-proof. "I'm not in the way of the buses. Let me sleep."

"Hey, be respectful," Jules growled from behind Wilma.

"You have to move down the hill." She put the sandwich and a juice box in his hands. "If you don't go, someone will take your place and you'll have to find a new spot to beg."

Marty put the sandwich and juice box in his pocket. "Fucking assholes will at that." He got up and shuffled off down the hill.

Moving through the trees, Wilma roused sleepers and

handed out food. Most of them grumbled but moved along. Jules stayed close behind, ready to step in if there was trouble.

The only other sleeper was on the other side of the circle around the statue. Wilma had two more sandwiches to give out, so she flicked the flashlight across the parking lot to be certain she hadn't missed anyone sleeping in the spaces, and then walked around to the far side of the circle.

"Wake up now." She strode over to the shape. "Hey, come on. Wake up. You need to move on."

She prodded the lump and the tattered grey overcoat slid off showing the naked body beneath. "Shit!" Wilma dropped the sandwich. She'd found bodies before, street people often died in their sleep, worn out from hard living. This was different. This body was not just a worn out human being. This body was mutilated.

In the glow of Jules' flashlight, she could see the color of the skin, off white with a slight blue tinge showing in the few places that were not marked with cuts and burns. The burns shaped in patterns of circles, the cuts were pentacles, and what seemed random slashes.

Wilma put her hand over her mouth and ran to the trees before she brought up her breakfast.

SEVEN

In the morning, her headache gone, Felicity decided to stay home for at least part of the day and catch up on work. If Sam Barton needed to ask her more questions, he could find her. Lists of her temporary staff with contact numbers and skills, covered her small dining table. She planned to make calls to all of them and update the information before going to the office to input it on the computer records. She knew she would be more efficient if she kept a laptop or a computer at home but having a pen in her hand and pad to doodle on helped her think.

From her seat at the dining table, she could see through to the trees lining the sidewalk across the road. She liked the sight of greenery. Her home held touches of both nature and her religion. A green man mask carved from a fallen oak branch, a pot of rosemary growing on the window ledge. It made her feel connected to an older world.

When she heard the creak of the front steps, Felicity assumed it was George, her downstairs tenant, returning home. His door was beside hers and opened on stairs that went down to the basement. She owned the entire house. Her section comprised the fully renovated main floor and a top floor that still waited for planning permission to make into another apartment.

Thinking she would invite George in for a coffee, she put down her pen and walked to the door. As she approached, she saw that the silhouette outlined on the frosted glass was too tall and solid to be George. Felicity peeked through the curtain covering the window facing the porch, and saw Sam's profile. She wanted to ignore him, but the problem with glass doors, frosted or not, people could see her move around in the house.

"Agent Barton." Felicity opened the door as she put on her business face. "Sorry, Special Agent Barton."

"Ms. Armstrong, good morning." He stepped forward before she could invite him in. Felicity reminded herself not to show her annoyance, as she stepped aside.

"Would you like some coffee?"

"No, thanks. I've already drunk a pot. I've been up since dawn."

She noticed the tiredness in his face, bags under his eyes, and tightness around his mouth. It adds a bit of character to his face, she thought, as a blush of attraction rose on her cheeks.

"Are you here to finish what we started last night?"

Sam shook his head and gestured to the couch. "No, it's not about that."

"What's happened?" Felicity couldn't look at Sam. She could feel the bad news in the air.

"The police found another body." He rubbed his hands through his hair and down the back of his neck as though trying to stretch the weariness out of his muscles.

Felicity looked up from her pile of manila folders. "I don't know what to say. I mean, I want to ask where, or who, but I don't think it would help. You have something else to say don't you." She saw his lips harden and his eyes focused on her face.

"Do you know anyone named Katherine Poole?"

"Yes, she's one of my temps."

"She was." Sam's eyes stayed fixed on her face. "Her body was found this morning, early this morning, on Telegraph Hill. When was the last time you spoke to her?"

Tears tightened Felicity's throat and built behind her eyes. She swallowed the pressure and wiped her eyes with her fingers. "It's been a couple of days."

Sam ignored her distress. "What happened when you saw her?"

She put her hand up. "Just a second. Please, just give me a second." The tears were building again. This time she let them fall. Pulling a tissue from the box on the side table, she pressed it to her eyes and breathed in and out slowly, trying to regain composure on each exhalation.

After what felt like hours, Felicity wiped her eyes one last time before looking up at Sam. He turned his gaze from the floor to her face, as though he'd sensed she was ready to talk. Tearing the tissue to shreds as she spoke, Felicity answered, "She'd had a fight with one of the people she was working for. She said the boss came on to her. I tried asking for details, but she accused me of not believing her and left. I've been trying to contact her today to see if she's calmed down."

"Did you believe her?"

"I didn't much care for the client, but I didn't want to jump to a conclusion." Felicity looked down at her hands, clasped tightly together in her lap, shreds of tissue showing between her clenched fingers. Now that she saw them, she could feel the pain from her nails digging into her skin. "I phoned him, and he said it was a misunderstanding. Then his assistant called me and told me that this was the fifth misunderstanding in six months. I cancelled the contract."

"Did anyone else work for this client?"

Felicity could see the tension in Sam's shoulders, his voice was even, but his body denied the calmness. "I'll check when I get into the office. I think so, but I don't remember who. We hadn't had the account long." She stood and grabbed her briefcase. "I'll go in now. Did you want to come?"

"I'll get the car." He strode to the door. "Meet me outside."

FELICITY USED the drive to get her emotions under control. As they pulled into the parking lot across the street from her office, Sam's BlackBerry rang.

"Barton," he snapped into the mouthpiece. "Now? Okay, where?" He closed the phone and turned to Felicity. "I have to go into the station. I'll come up when I'm done. It shouldn't take too long."

Felicity nodded as she opened the car door. "I'll start looking through the files. I should have the information ready by the time you get back."

As she crossed the street, Felicity fretted over the details she needed to pull from her files. She didn't want to involve Isaac in the search because she didn't feel up to his appetite for gossip. The information would be filed under the business name... F something.

She opened the door hoping that Isaac would be away from his desk. No luck.

"I thought you were working from home." He looked at her, eyebrow raised.

"I needed some information from the files. I'll be in my office if anyone wants me." She kept her voice light, trying to keep his suspicious mind calm. "If you can, try to give me some uninterrupted time. Oh, and good morning." She smiled and closed her office door.

"Okay," she mumbled. "Now, F what?" She typed her password into the log in screen and waited for the system to start up. When it was ready, she opened the client log and pulled up all the files starting with F. "Fox enterprises. There it is."

She read the details. *Owner, Stephen Fox; type of business, merchandizing,* no invoice dates. Without the invoice dates, she wouldn't be able to bring up the data or the names of the staff she'd assigned to the work. If the invoices weren't in the computer yet, Isaac was right; they really needed to get the files fully automated.

Not wanting to risk bringing Isaac into it, Felicity opened the file containing her employee records. "Maybe I made a note in Katherine's file," Felicity said, scrolling down the list of names.

She pulled up Katherine's file and checked the dates of her assignment to Fox Enterprises. Taking a pad of notepaper and pen from her desk drawer, she wrote down the details for Sam. She knew he could subpoena her files but preferred to give him information and try to keep her files confidential.

She wrote Katherine's name on the paper and the date of the assignment. She noted that Mr. Fox provided positive feedback. *Katherine completed her assignment quickly and accurately* according to the comments. *We would be happy to have her back.* That had different significance in light of the recent events.

There was nothing entered in the file about anyone else working at Fox Enterprises.

Felicity flipped back to the Fox Enterprises file to get the start date of the account. Fox was a recent client so she could probably cross off most of the names by looking at the calendar, which showed who was available, not who wasn't, another idea to add to the list of items that need integration.

His client account started six weeks ago, and Katherine worked for him last week. She opened the calendar and made a list of the fifteen people who had been looking for assignments in the first five weeks of the account.

After another half an hour of digging in records, she found that three of her temps worked there: Katherine, Amanda, and Kent. Kent was on assignment today, but Amanda was in the office. Felicity remembered hearing her voice coming from the kitchen earlier.

"Hey, boss." Isaac looked up from his salad bowl. "Are you done? We were talking about going for a drink after work, you want to come?"

"Maybe," she answered the second question. "I'm not finished, but I need to talk to Amanda. Is she around?"

"Yes. She went on a coffee run, but she should be back any minute."

"Great, I need to talk to her about an assignment she had." She filled her coffee cup with water from the cooler. "What's the occasion for the drink? Did I miss a birthday?"

"No, I wouldn't let you miss an important date. We decided we hadn't been out for a while and we're losing touch."

"You know, I like that idea, we should make a point of arranging a regular get together." With the recent events, Felicity realized that she'd allowed her team to drift away. These people were her family, this small group of people who worked full time hours at client locations, or in her office. There was a larger group of temporary staff. They came and went depending on school schedules, travel plans, or other personal priorities. But, Isaac, Amanda, Kent, and up to now, Katherine were her team, her friends, her family.

"You mean like a monthly team meeting?" Isaac's voice cut into her thoughts. "We could meet at a different new bar every month."

"You're on." She was relieved Isaac had something normal to focus on. He didn't know Katherine was dead, and that made him her safe haven. When he knew, and he'd gotten over his initial shock, he would start trying to guess who did it, coming up with all kinds of bizarre scenarios.

She heard the door buzz. Isaac set the alarm to notify them that the door opened whenever he stepped away from the front desk. Amanda came around the corner before the second buzz indicated the door closed.

"Felicity, I got you a latte just in case you were suffering from caffeine deprivation."

"Thanks." She appreciated the thought and at least it was more milk than caffeine. "Can you come into the office for a couple of minutes? I'm going through some files and I need some input from you."

Amanda put the cardboard tray down on the table and lifted out the frozen coffee drink. "Sure, did Isaac ask you about drinkies tonight? Do you think Katherine might come?"

"I don't think so." Felicity forced herself to sound normal. They'd tell everyone before the end of the day. In fact, Kent should be checking in at the office tonight because his assignment was over. If Sam could stay long enough, maybe they could both tell the team what had happened.

When they were in her office, Felicity showed the Fox Enterprises file to Amanda. "I noticed you were assigned to work there. Do you know anything about the owner, or any of the staff there?"

Amanda squirmed in her seat, a sure sign she'd been caught doing something wrong. Felicity waited patiently for her to talk.

"No, I didn't actually work there," she said, taking a sip from her frozen coffee.

"Why?" Felicity leaned forward. "And, more importantly who did? I know someone did because the client didn't complain."

"I'm sorry, boss." Amanda sat up straighter, "Kent told me he'd seen some stuff happening there that I wouldn't like."

"Why didn't you tell me?"

"I didn't want to put you in a position to lose a client."

"What did you do? Someone worked the hours."

"Katherine told me she knew a guy who needed the hours. She'd vetted him and said he could do the work. I swear I wouldn't have just sent someone without knowing he could do the job."

"So, you paid him directly?" Felicity needed to get as much detail as she could while Amanda was talking.

Amanda shook her head. "I paid Katherine, she paid him. Now I think about it, it's possible they were dating. Why don't you ask her?"

Felicity avoided answering the question. Amanda was going to find out soon enough why she couldn't ask Katherine. "Amanda, if you hear anything about a client you need to come to me. I'll check it out and figure out what to do. You're right about not wanting to lose clients, but we don't need business that puts our staff in difficult situations."

"Didn't Katherine work there after me?"

"Yes." Felicity looked down at the file in a pretense of checking the facts. Facts she already knew too well. "She told me what happened to her, and when I told her I'd check it out, she got angry and thought I should just believe her."

"Oh, I wonder why she didn't just send this guy along for her."

"I don't know. Anyway, I've cancelled the contract so no one will have to deal with it in the future." Felicity struggled with her instinct to tell Amanda about Katherine. She wanted to make sure the girl didn't feel any responsibility for what had happened. The only way she could do that was tell her the whole story. The problem was, she knew that the police would want to control the release of information.

"Look, don't worry about it. In the future just let me know if there's a problem." It felt like a cop-out, but it was the best Felicity could do.

"Okay." Amanda looked up into Felicity's face. "Are we okay with this? I mean, I'm sorry, I really am. I was only trying to help."

"We're fine. I'll talk to Kent when he gets in."

Amanda left and Felicity sank down into her chair. She couldn't throw off the feeling that she'd betrayed a trust. It felt cowardly not to walk back into the kitchen with Amanda and tell her and Isaac about Katherine's death. She knew that if she tried, the tears would start.

She pulled out Sam's business card and dialed the number.

"You've got the voice mail of Sam Barton, leave a message and I'll call you back."

"Sam, I have some details on the Fox Enterprises file. If you aren't coming by the office, give me a call."

EIGHT

An hour later, Isaac ushered Sam into Felicity's office. "I got your message," Sam said, sitting across from her.

"Cream and sugar?" Isaac called through the open door.

"Black," Sam shouted.

"Easy. Perfect, I like my men easy," the response came back.

Sam turned to Felicity. "So, what do you have for me?"

She handed him the paper with her notes on. "I checked the records. Other than Katherine, two people were assigned to work for Fox."

Sam scanned the notes and nodded. "I'll need to talk to them."

"I already talked to Amanda," Felicity admitted. She paused while Isaac delivered the coffee. "She switched her assignment with someone."

Felicity noticed the twist of his lips before he took a sip of coffee. She sat up straight bracing for a lecture.

"I wish you hadn't done that. It helps to see people's reactions."

"I know you want to control the situation, but these are my people. I haven't told them about Katherine, but they need to know, and it needs to be today." Felicity was ready to fight Sam if he disagreed on this point. If she couldn't control anything else, she would control how Sam treated her friends.

"How many people are your people?" Sam asked. The accompanying sigh was enough to keep Felicity on guard for a fight. "Until they're cleared, they are suspects, not your people."

"Have you cleared me? Am I a suspect?" She knew the answer but wanted to hear Sam confirm it. She would keep asking until she believed him.

"Everyone who isn't specifically cleared is a suspect at this point. Even the people who found the bodies, even the cop who found Katherine was a suspect. Some people are just easier to clear than others. So how many people are your people?"

"It's just three of them. Kent, he's on the list of people who worked for Fox. Amanda and Isaac are the other two. I know everyone says something like this, but I can't believe that any of them are capable of killing anyone."

"You're probably right. It looks like the killer is punishing people." He took a deep breath and ran his hands through his hair. "Tell me what you think your people would do to punish someone?"

Felicity pushed aside her annoyance at the way he emphasized 'your people'. "Kent, he'd just avoid getting into that kind of position. He's a Buddhist and really believes the teachings. I can't see him trying to punish anyone. He'd trust that they'd be judged in the next life."

Sam made notes. "Go on"

"This is too cold and calculated for Amanda. She'd fly off the handle and have a screaming fight with someone, and then it would be over."

"Are you sure? It's easy to hide the fact that you hold a grudge when you have a reputation for burning hot and fast."

"Oh, yes." Felicity smiled with the memory of Amanda's last

fury. "Her boyfriend dumped her in front of all the office staff. If she were going to punish anyone, it would have been him. He was a complete jerk. He'd been cheating on her. He thought it would be a good idea to come clean and tell her in front of her co-workers. He was wearing a designer suit. It looked like it cost a couple of thousand. She had a bowl of chicken curry in her hand. She threw it at him. It ended up all over his outfit. She somehow managed to make sure it hit everything he was wearing.

"Two days later he called to tell her that his mother had passed away. Amanda helped him arrange the funeral and supported him through the next couple of months while he was grieving."

"Okay, what about Katherine?" Sam asked.

"How can she be a suspect?"

"No, she's not, but she might have attracted the killer some way." He held up his hand as Felicity started to speak. She swallowed her anger and waited. "I know what you're going to say, but I'm not blaming her. Sometimes the only way to find why someone was a victim is to dig into their lives."

"She was hot tempered too." Felicity silently asked the Lord and Lady for wisdom. She understood Sam's point, but no matter how fairly Felicity tried to put it, it felt like she was betraying Katherine. "The difference is she would take a long time to cool down. The way she reacted to my questions about Fox Enterprises is a good example. Although, now I wonder if she wasn't feeling a bit guilty about deceiving me."

"Tell me again what happened."

"She came into the office at the end of her first day with them. She was obviously upset. I asked her what happened and she said Mr. Fox made some comments that were unnecessary. I asked for details and she told me that he'd commented on the nice way her sweater fit. She said it wasn't what he said, but how he looked at her when he said it."

"Then what?" Sam prompted as Felicity paused.

She thought back to the meeting, and her stomach clenched with the memory of Katherine's fury. "I said I'd look into it and she started yelling at me." Felicity paused, relaxing the anger holding her chest. "Accusing me of taking the client's side and valuing money over the wellbeing of my employees. It sounded weird at the time. Like she'd been scripted, but she was taking law classes, so sometimes she did sound like she was quoting a textbook. Anyway, I tried to calm her down and reassure her that I wouldn't do that, and she just swore and ran out the door."

Sam looked up from his notebook. "So, that's why you hadn't heard from her for a few days?"

"Yes. I was giving her some cooling down time. After the call from Mr. Fox's assistant, I cancelled the contract. I thought she would be able to get over it if I told her that. I guess I could have left a message, but I really wanted to talk to her in person."

"So, what about Isaac?" Felicity saw Sam's lips twitch upward.

"You really think Isaac could keep quiet about this if he was the murderer?" She laughed, feeling a little of the stress rise from her shoulders. "His version of punishing people is to give them the cold shoulder."

"Okay." Sam closed his notebook. "Look, I know you want your staff to hear what happened but let me do it. I need to see how they react, and I want to control what details go out."

She felt the tension completely leave her muscles. "I've been dreading it. I keep thinking someone will find out and come to tell me. I feel like a traitor."

Sam checked his watch. "Can you call them in so they're all together? I don't want to wait too long but I think it would be best to tell them all at the same time. That way I know they haven't talked to each other."

"What time is it?" Felicity asked.

"Five."

"Kent will be here in a few minutes. Isaac and Amanda have made plans for all of us to go for drinks so no one is going to be rushing out."

"I NEED to talk to each of you about anything you can tell me that might help catch the killer," Sam said into the silence after his announcement of Katherine's death.

Amanda looked down and swallowed before she spoke, "What," she choked the next words down and started again. "What would we be able to tell you that might help?"

"I won't know until we talk." He turned to Felicity. "Is there a place I can interview people?"

"Go ahead and use my office. I'll get a coffee run going. It looks like we are going to be here a while."

"Thanks." Sam looked around the group. "Please don't talk to each other about this until I've met with each of you."

"Is this the right procedure?" Kent asked. "Aren't you supposed to let us get a lawyer?"

Sam nodded. "You're right. Usually we'd split you up and put you in separate rooms. I thought it might be a bit easier on you if we did a quick fact finding first. You don't need a lawyer. I'm not arresting you. I'm just trying to fill in some of the gaps in our information about Katherine."

"Okay." Kent put down the glass of water he'd been sipping. "I'd better go first. I guess I probably knew her best."

· · ·

IN FELICITY'S OFFICE, Sam moved the two chairs to the same side of the desk. He sat facing Kent, and then put his notebook down. When he made the announcement, Sam had watched the pallor on Kent's face turn from healthy pale to dull and sickly grey.

Kent leaned back in the chair "I'm sorry. I just wasn't expecting anything like that." He took a deep breath. "Okay, I know you need some information. Let's get on with it. My grief isn't going to help find out what happened."

"You were her friend?" Sam asked, hearing the sympathy in his own tone.

"I guess so. She was difficult sometimes... with people..." Kent paused, wiping his hand across his face.

Sam waited.

Kent straightened in his seat. "She was always ready to take offense, but she really was a nice person underneath." He paused again. "It seems she wasn't well known here beyond the work, so I'm not really clear on what might be important."

"I'll ask my questions then you can tell me anything else you think I need to know, okay?" Sam picked up the notebook and flipped back a page to remind himself what Felicity had told him. "The last anyone seems to have seen Katherine was after her assignment with Fox Enterprises. You worked there; can you tell me exactly what happened?"

"Mr. Fox is a bit sleazy. He's kind of sad really, but I guess the women might have a different point of view."

Sam leaned forward in his seat. "Give me some details of what you saw."

"He always focused his eyes on the boobs. He always stood too close. Most of his female employees were used to him so they had their ways of dealing with it. You know, he paid really well so they wanted to keep their jobs."

"How bad was it?"

"Like I said it was more sad than bad." Kent shook his head. "I should have told Felicity what I saw, but I didn't think."

"Amanda was assigned there right after you." Sam scratched some notes on the pad then looked up. "Do you know what happened?"

"Yes, she switched out. I'd told her what to be prepared for, and she didn't want to put up with it."

"Do you know who she switched with?" Sam didn't hold out much hope that he would get new information. He pushed away the frustration he felt, knowing the best tips usually came from unexpected sources.

"Katherine got her new boyfriend to switch in." Kent paused, looking at his hands clenched in his lap. "I don't want to get Amanda into trouble. Felicity is a great boss, but she wouldn't like us switching with someone she didn't know."

"Do you know who this boyfriend is?"

"Katherine met him in night school class. She was taking some paralegal courses so she could get some higher paying temp work. They'd been going out for about a month, maybe a bit less."

"Did you meet him?"

"Not really." Kent stopped, a frown creasing his brow.

"What does that mean?" Sam knew he had something more to say, maybe something important.

"I think I saw him." Kent closed his eyes. "Katherine was meeting me for a drink after class, and I saw her come out of the building with a guy. He kissed her cheek and left. I was a block away, and by the time I got there, he was gone and I didn't think to ask any questions."

"What did he look like?"

"My height, more or less, but heavy. He was wearing a base-ball cap, so I didn't see what his hair looked like."

"Heavy?" Sam looked at Kent who kept his eyes closed.

"Yes, fat I guess. He might have been around two fifty." Kent opened his eyes. "I didn't really get a good look, sorry."

"Did she ever mention his name?"

"Not to me. I didn't want to ask questions because she's, I mean she was private, and I figured she'd tell me what she wanted me to know." He rubbed his face. "Amanda might know his name, or someone at Fox."

"So, is there anything I haven't asked that I need to know?" Sam held out hope. Sometimes this question gave the case a whole new direction.

"I don't know." Kent shrugged. "This was the first boyfriend I heard about, but I really only knew her for the six months I've worked here. She seemed happy."

"Thanks. If you do think of anything call me." Disappointed, Sam handed Kent a business card. "Let's see if that coffee is here."

IN THE LOBBY, Isaac followed Felicity through the door. "Here's your coffee, black just the way you like it." He handed the paper cup to Sam, his usual flirtation missing. "We got some muffins too. Do you want one?"

"Nothing, thanks." Sam took the coffee cup and asked Isaac to send Amanda in.

"Come on Kent, we'll plan a service for Katherine while we wait." Isaac put his free arm through Kent's and led him to the back room.

"How did it go?" Felicity asked.

"Katherine had a boyfriend," Sam said, watching her face.

"Oh," Felicity said, a slight frown crossing her forehead. Sam wasn't sure if it was puzzlement or annoyance. "Oh, do you think he might have done this?"

"There's always a chance, but there's nothing for us to work with yet. My gut says you know the killer and, since you don't know the mystery boyfriend, it's not likely to be him. But don't jump to conclusions about anyone." He nodded toward the kitchen. "You should get back there. I don't like that fact that they are unsupervised."

Felicity laughed. A full-throated sound that made Sam smile in response. He liked her more when she wasn't wound up with tension and fear. "Okay, I'll get Amanda," she said as she turned back to the kitchen.

"I HAVE SOME QUESTIONS," Sam said as soon as Amanda sat down. "But we're very sketchy on anything to do with this, so I'd appreciate it if you could tell me anything you think I need to know."

"Ask your questions first, we'll see if I have anything to add," Amanda said as if echoing his earlier statement. She sat with her arms crossed and kept her eyes fixed on Sam's face.

"Okay." He picked up the notebook again. "You switched jobs with Katherine's boyfriend?"

"Yes, although I didn't know he was her boyfriend. She just said friend."

"Did you meet him?"

"No. She told me she'd take care of everything." Amanda straightened. "I did get his name, Alan Smith."

"You paid him for the shift?" Sam paused while Amanda nodded. "Cash?"

"Yes, I gave the money to Katherine."

"Do you know why Katherine worked the shift at Fox when she knew why you didn't want to?"

"When she was assigned the job, I asked her if she wanted

to tell Felicity what was going on. She said that Alan told her nothing was wrong with Mr. Fox. He said that Kent must have been mistaken."

"What else do you know?" Sam realized that he wasn't going to get much more from Amanda than direct answers to his questions. He hoped by giving her an open question, she would have no choice but to expand on her answer.

"I know I didn't do this, and I'm certain none of my colleagues did it."

"You're probably right. I still need all the information I can get to help me find out who did."

"I also know that the FBI doesn't get involved in murder. Why are you asking these questions and not the local police?" Amanda leaned forward, eager for Sam's answer.

"I can't discuss that." Sam closed his notebook. "If you don't have anything else for me, please send in Isaac."

PROMISING to meet them at the bar for drinks, Felicity closed the door and turned to Sam. "Can you give me any news? Was Isaac any help? I know he's a flirt, but he does know what goes on around here."

"I shouldn't tell you anything," Sam said.

Felicity saw the glint in his eyes. "It's a bit late for that, don't you think?"

Sam laughed. "He didn't have anything new to add. I did get some information, but I need to follow up on it before it becomes public." He pulled on his coat. "I told them not to talk. Do you think you can make sure they don't?"

"To each other?" Felicity shook her head. "It's probably already too late."

"No, I expect they'll need to talk to each other to try to make some sense of this. In fact, if they talk, they might think of something useful. I really don't want them talking to the press or anyone else." He opened the office door and gestured for Felicity to go ahead.

"I'll do my best." She turned and locked the door to the office. "But I'm not guaranteeing anything."

NINE

The others had gone home after drinks, but Felicity felt the need to work, hoping it would relieve some of the stress. Returning to the office, she started reviewing and boxing files for storage. The pale lavender of her office walls usually made her feel calm. Tonight, it seemed depressingly grey. Piles of files on the teak credenza called for her attention. She sighed. No matter how much she tried, she couldn't keep up with the filing, even in normal times.

Her business was getting too big for her to keep doing the busy work. She was going to have to let Isaac take it on full time. And, busy work wasn't making any difference to the pain in her shoulders or her heartburn, or the sadness that lingered in the corners of her consciousness.

The sound of footsteps on the stairs interrupted her work only half an hour after she'd started. Her stomach tightened in panic, and then she remembered locking the door behind her and relaxed. The footsteps stopped outside the door, and she heard the rattle as someone tried the handle.

"Felicity," Sam's voice came through the door. "Are you there?"

"Hang on," she called, walking over to unlock it. "What are you doing here?"

"I came by and saw the lights from the street. I figured it must be you up here. You know, I would rather you didn't work alone at night." He took her arm and led her into the office after throwing the latch on the outer door.

Felicity felt his concern warm her, and a little of the tension ingrained into her muscles relax. "I need to work and the door was locked, so I was safe. Have a seat." She moved a box off the visitor's chair and sat across the desk. "I assume you want something."

"That's what our relationship has become? I only come by when I want something?" Sam smiled and Felicity felt heat in her cheeks.

"I wasn't aware we had a relationship. We'll have to work harder at it if it's going to be more than cop and suspect." Felicity tried to keep her voice light. She was flattered by the teasing, but still suspicious. Sam was being too open with her, unless she was permanently off the suspect list.

"I just wanted to bring you up to date on what we found." He sat back in the chair and smiled at her.

She noticed that he didn't dismiss her as a suspect.

"You get information fast. I thought it would take time."

"With this many bodies, we are allowed to be pushy about getting answers and information." Sam stretched before continuing. "We contacted Mr. Fox at home and asked him about his temps. He sweated a bit when we probed about certain behaviors, but he volunteered to show us the videos from his surveillance cameras."

"He has surveillance videos of his office?" Felicity grimaced. "Isn't that kind of creepy?"

"Yes, and dangerous for him too. If anyone decides to press charges about sexual harassment the evidence is on the tapes."

Sam rolled his eyes. "I guess guys who behave like sleazes aren't too bright. He keeps the tapes in his desk."

"What else was on the video?" Felicity didn't want to know any details about Mr. Fox's indiscretions, but she needed to know what Sam had seen. "Was the one with Alan Smith still available?"

"Yup. I don't think he reuses the tapes, he just keeps them on file. Anyway, Alan Smith worked only one day. He sat at the same desk during the whole shift, and all that shows up on the tape is the back of his head. What was visible matched Kent's description, but wouldn't help find the guy in a crowded room."

"So, no progress." She started to tidy the files on her desk, preparing to go home.

"I didn't say that." Sam picked her coat up from the back of the chair and held it out. "I did more than chat with Mr. Fox, I interviewed him. He has an alibi. He was working in a soup kitchen around the time we think Katherine was killed."

Felicity looked over her shoulder at him as she shrugged into the jacket. "You're kidding me."

"No. I guess even sleazes have a humanitarian side." He pulled open the door to the office and took her by the arm. "I'm parked across the street. I don't want you going home alone."

"Thanks, but let's not make this a habit. I'm not interested in explaining to my neighbors why I keep coming home with you."

Sam chuckled and put his arm around her shoulder. Felicity let it rest there; it made her feel safe.

TEN

After a restless night, Felicity met the morning with an extra prayer to the Lord and Lady, asking for help to stop the killer. She was rolling the carpet back over the circle in front of the fireplace when the doorbell rang.

What she wanted to do was go back to bed, but she knew that a few more hours spent staring at the ceiling wouldn't bring her any more rest than the last six had. What she did was draw a deep cleansing breath and turn to the door as she exhaled.

"Felicity, good morning." Sam stood in her doorway wearing a dark suit, his gun evident in the bulge on the side of his jacket. "Can I come in?"

"I'm sorry," she said turning aside. "Yes, of course, come in." The formality rose off him like aftershave clean, efficient, and brisk. "Coffee?"

"No, thanks." Sam looked around. "I have a few questions."

"Has something else happened?" The breath that should have brought calm to her was now shallow and tense. She waited to hear the news of another body.

"Yes." Sam's voice was cold. "I think we should go downtown to the police station."

"Why?" Felicity's stomach clenched. How bad could it be that she had to hear it at the police station?

"Just get your jacket, please." Felicity went to the closet and took her jacket off the hanger. She couldn't understand why he'd changed. He seemed angry and disappointed at the same time. What happened to the caring person who talked to her on the way home last night?

He waited on the porch while she locked her door, and then followed her to the car he'd left double-parked in the street. The drive to the police station was short, but the silence in the car made it seem like an eternity. The sunshine reflecting off the wet streets did nothing to lift her spirits.

SAM PARKED in the lot beside the station, and then directed her through the front doors, past the busy desk sergeant, and to a small office in the back of the building. She shivered. The room was stark, the walls bare and painted grey, the ceiling tiled with white panels randomly pierced with small holes, the only furniture, grey painted metal, chipped, and scratched.

She was now so tense she could feel the blood pushing through her body. Her pulse felt as though it was visibly shaking her frame. She closed her eyes and took a deeper breath telling herself that she could handle whatever was coming. "Sam, what's going on?" Her voice caught on the short sentence. Her throat was so dry with fear she felt it stick.

"Have a seat, please." He pointed to the metal chair. Felicity noticed it was bolted to the floor.

Felicity sat. "Sam, I don't understand."

"Ms. Armstrong, you told the police you were at home the night they found the body of Brian Wells."

"Yes. My neighbor can confirm that." The questions weren't

leading in the direction that Felicity expected. Sam wasn't talking about new victims. This was something else.

"The police asked Mr. George Thomas and he confirmed that he spoke to you that evening as you returned home." Sam took his notebook out of his pocket and laid it on the table.

"Am I being interrogated?" Felicity sat up straighter in the cheap metal chair. "It sounds like you didn't like what George told you."

"You aren't being interrogated. I need to clear up some details." Sam looked up from the notebook and stared at Felicity. "You said he was your neighbor."

"Yes, he lives downstairs." Everything about Sam that felt comforting and safe had turned hard and accusing. "If I'm not being interrogated, why am I in this room?"

He ignored her question. "We understand he rents the lower level of your home from you."

Felicity nodded. "For about five years."

"Do you have someone else who could provide an alibi?"

"Why?"

"Mr. Thomas receives a very good deal on his rent." Sam's eyes maintained contact with Felicity.

"Yes, I like to keep a good tenant, and George is a great one." She returned his stare. "Why am I here?"

"It's suspicious that your only alibi relies on you for such a sweet deal. Do you have anyone else who can confirm you were home?"

"No, but I think I might need a lawyer now." She stood and leaned toward Sam, bracing herself with her hands on the cold tabletop.

"I said you weren't being interrogated. I can call someone for you if you really want a lawyer." He stepped closer, looming over her.

"If I'm not being interrogated why do I feel as though I am?

What do you have that makes you think I could possibly kill someone? Let alone kill this many people."

"Nothing." Sam stated a fact, no emotion, no inflection. "But then we have nothing to make us know you wouldn't."

"I thought we were working together, that we trusted each other." Felicity could feel her anger and stress start to take control again. She kept her voice low as she spoke, hoping to project a sense of reason. "You forced me to round up my staff so you could question them."

"Yes." He nodded. His emotions clearly in better control than hers.

"I don't even know most of these people. Two of the poor victims, two that's all I knew." She leaned farther across the table getting in Sam's face. "Yesterday we were a team, and today I'm here. What's changed?"

"Your alibi," Sam said.

"Give me strength," she said through clenched teeth. Her grip on her temper rapidly slipping. "I don't have another alibi. I told you. I picked up some dinner and went home." She could feel her body shake against the anger she struggled to keep leashed.

"Do you have a receipt for the food?" Sam didn't rise to the fury boiling from her, nor did he back away as she leaned into his space. "The people at the restaurant don't remember you coming in that day."

"Enough!" She slammed her palm flat on the metal table, letting her temper take over in the face of the icy calm Sam presented. Feelings of hurt and betrayal rose from her gut like fire. She thought they were becoming friends, maybe more than friends.

As suddenly as it had risen, the heat burned out. Her grief over the killings and the lack of sleep combined to fade her vision to grey and leave her cold. "I said, enough," she said wearily. "I'm leaving."

"Felicity, I'm sorry." She heard kindness in his voice again. "Look, my specialty is finding and stopping serial killers. The cops don't know how to handle this type of case."

"So, you think I might be a serial killer?" Felicity sat down shocked. She realized she'd missed that connection, but didn't serial killers have rituals? Didn't they take trophies or something?

"You are linked to more than one of the bodies." Sam shrugged. "I'd be stupid not to think you might be a good suspect."

"I'm going home." Felicity stood but the strength of the emotions over the last few minutes had drained her. She swayed and sat back down.

"Wait." Sam held up a hand, palm out. "I know you're pissed, but you're also in no shape to go home by yourself. Let me get you some water, and when you've got yourself together I'll take you home."

Felicity nodded. She thought, *a glass of water is fine, but you aren't driving me anywhere.*

SAM STOOD with his back to the interview room door. He needed a minute before going into the bullpen and talking to Morton and Kang. He hated treating her like this. He had to follow procedure. It didn't matter that he knew she was innocent. Interrogating her would also clear her with the cops.

He pushed away from the door and walked into the bullpen.

"Okay, Kang, give her a few minutes then take in a glass of water," Sam said, and then sat on the desk shared by the two detectives. He was still officially assisting the police in the investigation. It wouldn't be long before he would have to take it over.

Their first meeting hadn't been promising. The body that kicked off this investigation had been their case.

"What do you think?" Bobby Morton looked up at Sam. "You think she's involved?"

"No." Sam picked up a pen and started spinning it as he spoke. He tried to ignore the feeling in his gut that he was damaging his relationship with Felicity beyond repair. He'd let too much go because he liked her. "I don't, never did. I had to push it though, so we could all cross her off the list."

"You aren't going to drop her as a suspect, are you?" Bobby took a drink from his coffee cup.

"She's involved somehow, but I don't think she knows it. I need to get her back on my side. I think she knows something, but I'm not asking the right questions. Whatever it is, it's not coming up." He put the pen down. It would be a pleasure to stick close to Felicity.

"Why are you here alone?" Bobby changed the subject. "I mean you Feds work in teams. In fact, we usually don't get a look in when the Special Agents hit town. Why are you working with us?"

"My partner's in the hospital and my director thought I could use some sensitivity training with the locals." Sam nodded his head toward the two detectives. "Apparently, I have a habit of upsetting overly sensitive detectives."

Bobby laughed. "I'm surprised that is an issue at the FBI, isn't it like a lesson in how to be an agent 101?"

"Yeah," Kang added as he returned from dropping off the glass of water. "You know, if we work together we might be able to deflect to you some of the crap that usually rolls down to us."

"Gee, thanks." Sam got back to the subject at hand. "How was she?" He was surprised at how much the answer meant to him.

"Quiet. I think she was meditating or something when I came in."

"Okay, time to start again. This time I need to make repairs."

"How does that work?" Bobby Morton asked. "I can't get my wife to forgive me even when I haven't done anything wrong."

"Ah, that's the problem, Morton. You don't realize you've done something wrong. You need to remember you have always done something, you just don't know what it is." Sam slapped Kang on the shoulder as he left.

Opening the door to the interview room, Sam saw Felicity sitting with her elbows on the tabletop, her head in her hands. The pose made her auburn hair fall straight to the desktop.

"Felicity, I still need to ask you some questions." He pulled out a chair and sat across from her. At the sound of his voice, she pushed back her hair and sat up straight.

"Before you start I need to say something," she said.

"I think it would be better for you to answer my questions. Did you think of another alibi?" Sam placed his notebook on the table.

"No, not for that night, but..." She paused and seemed to be gathering her words.

"Okay, let's get on with it, then."

"Sam, you can't really believe I did this... killed these people."

"It's not about what I believe. I have to follow procedure."

"I know. I'm trying to tell you..."

"Felicity, I think we're almost done. If we can get through a few more questions, I can take you home."

"Damn it Sam, I'm trying to apologize," she snapped, and then threw up her hands. "I'm sorry. I don't like losing control. My temper got the better of me before, and that wasn't fair." Her gaze dropped to her lap

"Okay." Sam flipped the pages of his notebook to keep her from seeing the relief her words gave him.

"I can only explain it as grief. Over the last week, I've seen and heard some awful things." She leaned forward. "I know you're just doing your job, and I'll try to be more helpful."

Sam saw the lines around her eyes and mouth. It looked like she hadn't slept for a week or more. "You must be exhausted. I hope it's going to get easier from this point forward. If we can get clear on your alibis for the approximate times of the murders, we can start looking at other suspects."

"Okay, I'll try to help." She rolled her shoulders as if to relax them and clasped her hands in her lap.

"We have five bodies. It looks like Brian and David were killed about the same time, maybe a day apart. You've already told us what your alibi is for the 23rd evening, and your staff confirms you were in the office all day. If you can give us some idea of where you were early in the morning that should deal with two victims." Sam looked at her expectantly.

"What day of the week was that?"

"Thursday."

"I was at a Chamber of Commerce breakfast meeting from 6:30 am to eight and went straight to the office from there. You can talk to anyone who was at the meeting. I'll give you some names and phone numbers if you'll pass me my purse."

Sam handed the purse from where it rested on the back of the third chair in the room. Felicity pulled out her BlackBerry and gave him the names of three people who were at the meeting. He left and asked Bobby Morton to make the calls.

"Okay, as far as we can tell the next person was killed on the 28th," Sam said, entering the room.

Felicity brought up the calendar on her BlackBerry. "Tuesday, I have nothing in the morning, let me think." She tapped her finger on the screen to move the display through the day.

"Yes, I stopped to pick up bagels at Holes for breakfast. We had a rush job in the office for a client. Amanda, Isaac, and I worked through to about midnight then shared a cab home."

Sam wrote the information down and asked, "Which company?"

"Bay Area Taxi. We have an account."

"The next date is August 31. The coroner thinks it was in the evening. Lila hadn't been dead long before she was found."

Felicity switched dates in the calendar. "Last Friday. That evening I volunteered at the Green Fayre. I was facilitating discussions on ways to reduce our carbon footprint." She looked up at Sam. "The event started at three and went until about nine. I'm sure the organizer can give you some contact information from the participants of the three sessions to confirm I was there."

Sam noted the name of the organizer. "What did you do afterwards?"

"I was pretty tired." Felicity closed her eyes to picture the evening. "I rented a movie and picked up a pizza."

"What movie?"

"*Rabbit Proof Fence*, you can check the rental place at the end of my street; it's called MovieTime."

"Was it good?" Sam smiled, trying to repair the damage he'd done at the beginning of the interview.

"Yes, enough to keep me awake despite the fact I didn't get much sleep the night before." Felicity smiled back, apparently willing to give a bit of forgiveness.

"Katherine seems to have been killed and dumped right away." He watched as the grief returned to Felicity's face. "Do you have an alibi for early this Thursday?"

Felicity took a deep breath and clenched her hands against the guilt and grief that flooded her. "No, I was at home alone." Tears gathered in the corner of her eyes. She pulled a tissue from her purse. "I think George might have seen me come home, but he wouldn't know if I stayed in or not."

"Okay. Look, stay here and wait while we verify some of this. I'll take you home when we're done."

SAM SAT on a corner of Kang's desk while he waited for the final confirmations to come in. He hoped his relationship with Felicity would survive this, or more than survive.

"Why do I think you want to let her off the hook?" Kang asked. "And, that chair is free, it might be more comfortable."

Sam hooked the chair closer and sat. "I don't know why you think that."

"She's pretty hot. Are you using something other than your brain to make decisions?"

"No." Sam hoped he was telling the truth. "I'm following procedure here. Do you have any problem with it? You not happy with the level of interdepartmental cooperation?"

"Yeah. I see you going through the motions. If it's not your... heart running the show, how do you know she's not a suspect?" Kang sat back in his chair sipping office coffee from a paper cup. He grimaced and added another pack of sugar.

"Probably the same way you do," Sam said, knowing the trick for every investigator is to get comfortable with the fact that you never completely clear anyone during an investigation, no matter how much you want to.

"Gut and percentages, then." Kang put the coffee down. "My gut says she couldn't have done it. Unless something changes, I say if we get enough confirmation on her alibis, we move along."

"Well, a bit more than that." Sam counted on his fingers. "One, I don't think she pressured her tenant into providing an alibi. His story didn't sound rehearsed. Two, if she was at work or, Chamber functions, she wouldn't have had enough time to carry out these murders. They are complex, and you need time to do that much damage to someone. She looks tired but not that tired, if you get me."

"Yep and here's the answers." Bobby Morton put down the phone. "Four people confirmed she was at the Chamber meeting. Seems she arrived a bit early and left with everyone else."

"Okay, anyone else answer?" Sam made some notes in his pad.

Bobby flipped a page. "I talked to the organizer of the conference, and he said that he saw her at the beginning and end of each session. He gave me some names I can check with."

"She didn't have time to kill anyone while a session was on unless she did it nearby," Sam said.

"Call the attendees and let me know, but I'm thinking she can go." Sam put his own notebook away. "I gotta say I'm glad. Something says I will get more out of her if she's helping, than if I have to keep her as a suspect."

He stood, walked over to the interrogation room, and opened the door. "I'm driving you home," he said and saw the relief in her eyes.

ELEVEN

After Sam dropped her off, Felicity crawled back into bed. The interview had drained the last few drops of energy from her, including the edginess that kept her awake the last few days. Whatever she needed to do could wait a few hours.

When she woke, it was evening and her stomach was growling. Feeling rested for the first time since the police asked about her business card, she showered, pulled on jeans and a tee shirt, and decided to pick up a takeout dinner and go into the office. She needed to check the accounting for last month's billing and close the books off. She loved her business, but lately it felt like she lived at the office. When this was over, she would take a vacation, a long one.

She took a cab to Sushimi to pick up sushi and then headed to the office.

After verifying that the outstanding bills were correct, she signed them and put the papers in Isaac's inbox for him to mail on Monday. Still feeling energetic, she started clearing files out for storage. About half an hour and six paper cuts later, she flipped through the file labeled Tompkins, Ward. This was some transcription and database work completed for a non-fiction book. There was a pale-yellow sheet of paper in the back of the file. Felicity turned it over and started reading.

THIS ONE WANTED HELP *but when he saw your name, he said he would not take aid from a woman. Now he won't be hiring anyone ever again. Lord and Lady turn your backs. He slighted your aspect on earth.*

SWEAT CRAWLED from her body leaving behind shivering wet skin. This was about the body found at the Palace of Fine Arts – the one with her card. Felicity picked up her phone and called Sam.

"Barton," he barked as a greeting.

As she told Sam what she'd found, Felicity could suddenly feel all the empty space around her.

"I'm on my way." Sam hung up without waiting for her to speak.

IN THE TWENTY minutes it took Sam to drive over to her office, Felicity found two more notes. The first in a file of a long-time client. The contact's name was Lila Rose. Felicity remembered that the woman they found at the same place as David's body was Lila Rose.

SHE TOOK *credit for lovely Amanda's idea and got a promotion. Amanda won't be called back. This one cost you a client.*

Lord and Lady turn your backs. She betrayed your aspect on Earth.

SHE FOUND the third note in one of the empty files she kept on hand. This note puzzled her. It didn't fit anyone she knew.

THIS ONE PREFERRED *her voice to your needs. She should have sold you those shoes. She'll never sell again.*

Lord and Lady turn your backs. She shunned your aspect on Earth

FELICITY WAS PULLING out the last of her files when she heard knocking on the door. She'd been so preoccupied with the search that she hadn't heard footsteps on the stairs.

"Felicity, open up," Sam's voice came through. "Are you okay?"

"I'm coming." Her fear diminishing at the sound of his voice. She dropped the files back in the drawer and ran to open the door.

"I found two more notes," she said, her voice breaking.

"Have you touched them?" Sam asked. He took her arm and pulled her close. She resisted the urge to curl into the hug. When she stepped back, he said, "I mean, how much did you touch them?"

"The first one will probably have my fingerprints on the right-hand side." Felicity pointed to the paper on the left corner of her desk. Noticing her hand shaking, she pulled it back and wrapped her arms around her body. "I didn't realize at first what it was, sorry."

"No problem." Sam stood over the notes reading them. "What about the others?"

"I used my fingertips. My nails really." Felicity stood back while Sam looked around the office.

"Good." He nodded. "The files?"

"I've put them on the top of the cabinet. They will have lots of fingerprints on them. Most of my staff do filing from time to time." She pointed to the open drawer, her hand steadier. "I was almost finished."

"We'll go through the rest. I'll call my team in to check the office for fingerprints, trace, everything." He led her outside the office and down to the kitchen, arm around her shoulders.

"Are you sure you're okay?"

"No, but I'm not going to faint either, don't worry." Felicity's skin felt clammy, and she was chilled, so she wasn't sure she could keep that promise.

Sam looked at her and shook his head. He went to the fridge, pulled out a carton of orange juice, and poured a glassful. "Drink this. I don't think whoever it belongs to will mind."

The dizziness went away after she drank half the juice. "Thanks." She smiled at him.

"This is probably a safe place to hang out while we wait. It's too public to give us any useful evidence." He guided her to the sofa. "Have a seat while I call."

Sam pulled out his BlackBerry and pressed one button. "Mike? It's Sam Barton. Yes, I've been in town a few days. No, I've been working with the local PD on these murders. Yes, I'm taking the case over and we'll handle it from here out. It's definitely serial. Ritual, repetition, and now it looks like we've got a focus." He asked Mike to send the crime scene team to Felicity's office and hung up.

"Do you know what the notes mean? The signature in particular?" he asked.

Felicity nodded. "The Lord and Lady reference is Wiccan. Our religion has nothing to do with this though."

"Our religion?" Sam turned around from the counter where he'd been preparing a pot of coffee.

"Yes, I'm a believer in Wicca." She heard her voice rise with the words, a familiar need to defend her belief rose through feelings of weakness. "Whoever is doing this is twisting my belief into something evil. There is no aspect on Earth of the Lord and Lady, except symbolically in certain rites. That's for the high priest and priestess, though, and I'm not a high priestess. I think this person is probably just making it up as they go along."

"Okay, you don't need to defend your belief to me." Sam put his hands up in surrender. "What about this Vera Lau? The note doesn't match any of the bodies."

"I've been trying to think who it might be." Felicity relaxed and nodded in acceptance of Sam's raised coffee cup. "A few weeks ago, I was shopping in a little store on the Haight and the sales person ignored me. She was on the phone with her boyfriend. I finally gave up and left the store. That's all I can think of. I didn't know the name of the girl."

Sam passed her a mug of coffee. "What was the name of the store?"

"ReNew. It has vintage and current fashions."

"We'll check it out." He noted the information. "It seems we have at least one more body."

Felicity sipped her coffee. "Sam, you should know that thirteen is an important number for Wicca. We need to catch this person soon. There are five, maybe six bodies already."

"If he's using some aspects of Wicca what else might be important?" Sam sat on the chair and put his coffee mug down. He laid his notebook open and waited.

"The new moon is on the 22nd and it's Mabon, that's a day of celebration of the harvest and recognition of the coming winter. It is a powerful time for Wiccans." Felicity watched as Sam made notes. They both turned toward the front door when the sound of boots climbing the stairs announced the arrival of Sam's team.

TWELVE

It was dark outside. Inside, the room was lit with only a few flickering fluorescent rods. The man moved through the room, feet shuffling, head down. The sound of his shoes as he moved across the bare floor was like a hundred voices whispering secrets in the corners.

The room was square and unadorned except for a circle half blurred out in the center of the floor. The man was dressed in grey sweatpants and a grey hooded sweatshirt, the drabness of his clothes matched by the drabness of his skin and hair. He was pale and dull as though he had been ill or out of the sun for a prolonged period. His hair was a lifeless faded red and it hung straight down the sides of his face. He muttered quietly while he walked.

"It's time," he said, opening a door in the back of the room. "It's time to bring her closer."

In the room, stood a table covered with bottles and boxes. On a shelf above the table lay a folded cloth and two boxes of candles, one black and one white. Laid against the box of black candles were four disposable lighters, red, blue, white, and green. A book stood alone on a second shelf. The binding of the book was blood-red leather finished in a rough texture.

He took the book down, opened it at the page marked by a crimson ribbon. He placed the book on the table and pulled a cheap ballpoint pen from the pocket of his sweatshirt.

"She will have to see me if she's alone." He reached for a box of grainy dust and shook some into a cracked white cup. He added liquid from a tall square bottle. The powder turned black in the liquid. From a small wooden box, he took a needle wrapped with thread.

"This one will cry in pain. I need the power of her tears to reach the Lord." He took a double-edged knife from its black velvet sheath and put it with the other items in the center of the circle. He returned to the small room at the back.

"A poem," he said as he picked up a stiff white sheet of paper.

"DON'T DESPAIR, don't cry my Lady
    I will come when the time is right
    When others leave my Lady
    I will bring you the light
    This is the first I give you
    She should not have told you lies
    I'll make her pay before she dies
    A friend she said and true
    But she lied to you."

AS HE SPOKE, he scratched the words on heavy paper with the cheap pen. "There, much nicer than the others. She will like this. I'm sure."

When he was done, he folded the paper and set it aside.

Taking a bottle of olive oil and a thick stick of white chalk back into the larger room, he placed them to the side of the blurred circle.

Smiling, he drew a five-pointed star on his right forearm with the pen. When he was done, he dipped the thread in the black ink, and began piercing his skin in a circle around the star.

Later, he walked to the dark far corner of the room where a metal stairway the color of the walls led up to a grey metal door. To the casual observer, neither door nor staircase would have been visible. He felt his way up the familiar steps, took a large black metal key from his pocket and opened the door.

The corridor beyond was lit by a series of small skylights. More a room than a corridor, it ran the full length of the building but was narrow. There was only space for a walkway and a desk, chair, and credenza against the wall all the way at the other end. Behind the credenza was another door, painted to match the walls.

The man rubbed his eyes as they reacted to the sudden change in light. It was night but there was glare from the moon pouring into the narrow space. He shuffled along to the end, pulling open the door and feeling inside for a light switch. He looked around the space and smiled at the emptiness and cold smell of cleanser. The old janitor had used all the closets, at one time or another, for storage.

Shutting off the light and closing the door, he opened a drawer in the credenza and laid a cup, saucer, and knife on the metal desk beside it. Then he pulled a small laptop computer from another drawer and pressed the power key.

He took a bottle of water from the credenza and drank half of it in one long desperate swallow. He poured the rest into the cup then entered a password on the laptop.

From the desk drawer, he took a small apple, and granola

bar. He used the knife to pare and slice the apple and placed it with the unwrapped granola bar on the saucer.

Sid Parker pulled a wooden stool from under the desk and sat down to plan his next murder while eating his meager dinner.

"Hmm, which ritual will be most appropriate," he mumbled through a bite of granola bar, before clicking on a file labeled full moon and starting his browse through the document.

September is the harvest moon. Time to realize the goals, or at least set them in motion for quick realization, he read.

Biting into the apple, he smiled at the idea that bubbled out of his subconscious. He would use spices to burn her. Burning cinnamon sticks to brand the skin, and mace to bind her. The signs he would carve would be of the moon and wheat and corn and other harvests. Each symbol would be rendered just short of full readiness. Each a few days from full ripeness.

The fruition of his goal should be at Mabon, not this night.

Sid made some notes on the moon rituals and noticed the time display in the lower right corner of the screen. It was time to get his victim. He shut down the laptop and put everything away.

THE DOORWAY across the street from the restaurant was shadowed, the store shut for the night. Sid shrugged his old dirty overcoat closer around his shoulders. The usual night chill had risen from the water an hour ago. His victim was sitting at a table in the window of the restaurant. She and her date had just ordered dessert.

A homeless person wandered by with a shopping cart full of empty cans. He, or possibly she, tried to step into the other side of the doorway. Sid growled, kicked, and ranted. His hopeful roommate muttered, "Peace, brother," and wandered on.

Despite the anticipation of the ritual to come, the cold made Sid drowsy, and as usual, when he felt sleep coming, he heard the sound of his grandfather's voice. "Boy, come here." It was the first thing the old man said when the social workers dropped Sid off at the old house. "You know what happened to your parents?"

"Yes, sir." Sid kept his eyes on the toes of his tennis shoes. "They went away with Reverend Jones."

"Know where?" Grandpa packed some tobacco in his pipe, "I said, do you know where?"

"Yes, sir, Guyana." He sucked in his lower lip and bit it to stop the tears.

"Drank that damn Kool-Aid. Damn fools." Grandpa reached out and raised Sid's chin. "Do you believe in the Reverend Jones, boy?"

"No, sir."

"Good." He patted the bench beside him. "Sit here and we'll talk about a real religion, boy."

Sid lived with his grandfather until the old man died. When grandpa got too senile to look after him, Sid pretended everything was fine so the social workers wouldn't put him in a foster home.

Grandpa had been a believer in Wicca. He told Sid that he bought a book and when he'd finished reading it, it made more sense to him than the bible ever did.

Sid remembered Grandpa showing him how to build a ritual to ask for a good crop or a healthy calf. Sid also remembered when a neighbor had taken a switch to him and beaten him until blood ran. Grandpa performed a ritual to bring sickness to the neighbor's house, thinking it was a just punishment.

Sid started to believe in Grandpa's ways when the neighbor was driven off in an ambulance to have his appendix removed.

A few months after that, Grandpa started to be confused.

Sid stopped going to school so he could take care of Grandpa. The school was in another county, and he told the principal they were moving away so they wouldn't come looking for him. His education became about spell casting and rituals.

When Grandpa died, Sid went to the lawyer's office for the reading of the will. The lawyer explained that Grandpa had been eccentric. Sid looked up the word later; a word used to describe weird rich people. Sid hadn't realized that Grandpa was rich, hadn't thought about money much at all.

The lawyer said Grandpa left Sid three million dollars on one condition. Sid had to finish school and go to college. Getting the education was the easy part. Learning to survive away from the farm was the hardest part.

Sid earned a degree in comparative religion. His perspective on the Jonestown Massacre and Jim Jones earned him high marks in a course on new religions. The same course challenged his understanding of Wicca. The teachers had it all wrong. He knew it was wrong that they said it was new. It must be an old religion, Grandpa talked about how the ancient people worshiped the Lord and Lady. It was wrong about spells too, saying it was dangerous to curse people, saying bad stuff came back three times. Grandpa wouldn't have taken the chance with the neighbor if that were true.

Sid felt a pain stab his back and realized he was bent over with his arms wrapped around his belly. The pain in his guts that always came when he remembered the past, tearing into his body, and dragging him back to the present.

He blinked to clear the tears from his eyes, and to get rid of the glare from the streetlights. He looked at the restaurant window again. She was gone.

His fear that he had lost his quarry while he was over-whelmed by memory sent another blade of pain through his body. He blinked again, and saw the woman standing at the door pulling on her coat.

The pain subsided. He felt calm fold over him like a warm blanket. This was the right feeling. This was how it always felt when the ritual started. It started now.

She parted from her date and walked alone to her home three blocks away. Sid kept up the image of a homeless man as he shuffled along after the woman

MUCH LATER THAT night Sid stood in a tub of warm water using a cloth to rub the gore and sweat off his skin. The water in the tub was pink and getting darker as Sid got cleaner. The streaks of clean skin were growing as though a tide was slowly ebbing.

He shivered in the cold air of the warehouse. His reaction to the cold and the pleasure of the completed ritual. Sid breathed in the smell of a successful rite, burned candles, oil, herbs, and flesh. The body lay in the center of the, now broken, circle. Relaxed in death like a child sleeping. The woman had fought the inevitable. Her fear strengthening the energy of the spell.

Sid stepped out of the tub onto a clean towel – white the color of purity. He reached over to the clothes hanging on the back of the grey metal chair. Sid didn't have to worry about soiling the clothes when he moved the body. It had no more blood to lose.

He went to a far corner of warehouse and dragged out a roll of bubble wrap. He pulled it until a large sheet flopped to the floor, then cut it. Stepping over the blurred lines of the circle, Sid bent and lifted the body by the shoulders to drag her onto the wrap. After he rolled her into it and sealed the bundle with duct tape, Sid pulled on a grey trench coat, lifted her onto his shoulders, and walked out into the night.

THIRTEEN

Felicity picked up her BlackBerry and redialed Amelie's number. They were meeting for dinner but Felicity needed to buy some more time before they met. Dealing with the investigation put her so far behind in her paperwork that it felt like she had to squeeze an extra ten minutes' production into every hour.

"Hey, Amie, give me a call," she said after the beep. "I need you to meet me at the office not the restaurant."

She ended the call, and then searched her contacts for Amelie's home number. "Hey, I left this message on your cell. Call me. I need to meet you at the office."

She hit the end call button and dropped the phone in her purse. Felicity sighed. It was odd for Amelie not to be answering the phone. A shiver ran across her shoulder blades and she made a prayer to the Lord and Lady that Amelie was all right.

Pulling the next file off the stack on her left, Felicity opened it and sorted the documentation into chronological order. When she and Sam had rifled the files looking for notes, they paid no attention to tidiness. They had shaken documents loose and stuffed them back into the folders with speed in mind, not accuracy. "I hate filing," she muttered, hoping it would be the last time she needed to reorder the paperwork.

Felicity flipped through files for two hours, occasionally reaching out for one of the alphabetized piles of papers to add to the contents of the open folders. She had worked from Ames to Peterson by early afternoon, then closed the Peterson file with a sigh. Her back was stiff from the unaccustomed stillness. Her fingers were nicked with paper cuts and dry from the constant rubbing against the paper. She sorted documents into alphabetical order from the chaos on the floor. The papers were now tucked safely into the right folders, hole-punched, and secured by clips. A small celebration of paper dots scattered across the desk and floor from the hole-punch.

As she stretched, Felicity heard her neck pop as the muscles pulled the bones into place. Then she reached into her purse for her BlackBerry. Amelie still had not returned her call. She pressed the speed dial for Amelie's cell phone and got her voicemail after four rings. "Same message as before, hon," she said. "Call me." Felicity called Amelie's home number and left the same message on the answering machine again.

The shiver she had felt earlier ran deeper into her gut. Felicity knew in her heart that something was seriously wrong. Amelie always returned her messages. Calling Amelie's work was usually fruitless. The private investigator she worked for didn't allow personal calls, and protected his employees, so no one would give her information about Amelie. She dialed the number anyway. The receptionist answered.

"Hi, can I leave a message for Ms. Singh, please."

"Yes, but she won't get it today." The voice was young and earnestly professional.

"Oh, why?" Felicity felt her stomach tighten.

"She isn't in the office today." Felicity could hear a hesitation in the voice.

"Is she at a meeting?" It was worth finding out how much more information she could get before corporate policy took over.

"I can't give out information on her." A now controlled voice quoted office protocol.

"I'm her friend. I've been leaving messages everywhere for her." Felicity could hear the panic in own her voice. "She's not answering. Just tell me that her absence was expected, so I can stop worrying."

"I can't do that." The voice paused. "I think I need to let the supervisor know what you've told me. Will you hold?"

"No. I'm calling the police." Felicity answered, and then dialed Sam's number. Police, FBI, whatever, she wanted someone with authority, and Sam was the highest authority she knew.

FOURTEEN

Detective Kang looked away from the body sprawled in the handicapped parking spot in Candlestick Park. The marks on the body turned his stomach. He said a quick thanks to whoever ran the universe that he'd passed on breakfast.

"Damn," Bobby Morton said through barely moving lips. Kang could see the muscles clenched on his partner's jaw. "It's another one. What the hell is this guy's kink? Why'd he drop this one at the Stick?"

Bobby's question pushed him to try to answer, "Maybe he doesn't like baseball." He looked at the body. The skin was whiter than most corpses he had seen. It looked like there was no color left, no blood. At least there was no blood spread around the body. "Killed somewhere else."

"Yes." Bobby nodded his head to encompass the entire corpse. "Somewhere isolated, that kind of damage causes a lot of noise."

"God, I hope the poor bugger was drugged," Kang said, thinking it unlikely. Someone who does this kind of damage does it for the pleasure. "Maybe he made a mistake, there's cameras all over the place here. We could get lucky."

"I'll get the security company to send us whatever they got."

"Who's coming to release the body?" Kang asked.

"Laura's off duty today, thank God." Bobby grimaced. "I know she's the pathologist, but she's also my wife. I hate when she has to see this stuff. I feel like I have to keep her protected from this kind of thing. I think it's the new man. I forget his name."

Kang nodded toward the man standing beside a pickup truck with two uniformed officers. "Let's talk to this guy while we wait."

Manuel Santoro's face was grey and shiny. His big hands clenched and unclenched, his body rocking slightly from side to side.

"I thought it was trash," he said in response to Bobby's request to tell them what happened. "I check the grounds before the games. There's usually something to clean, or fix, before we get ready to open for the game." He closed his eyes and swallowed. "I go over there, okay." He raised his chin in the direction of the body. "I didn't realize what it was right away. Jesus have mercy, it didn't look human, all those cuts and burns."

"Did you see anything else?" Kang asked.

"No, okay." Manny ran the back of his hand over his eyes. "Nothing. All I can see is this body with arms and legs all going the wrong way." He swallowed again. "Jesus, you think he lived through all that?"

"Hard to say." Kang made a few notes in his book. "Hard to say until they do the autopsy."

"Those cuts," Manny whispered. "They look like zodiac signs."

"You know who might have been here last, and when?" Kang asked.

"Who knows how many kids hang out here? Look, officially

the grounds manager probably was the last one here yesterday. He probably went home around eleven last night."

"His name?"

Kang wrote down the name.

"Kids hang out here most nights. Sometimes a gangbanger or drug dealer, if you guys moved them along from someplace else."

"Thanks." Bobby took a counseling service card from his wallet. "You might want to talk to someone at this number. Seeing this kind of stuff is hard to get over."

"Maybe." Manny took the card and held it close to his eyes to read it, "Victim's services?"

"Yes. They help people who are involved in traumatic crime. Call them. No cost."

The two detectives turned at the sound of the coroner's SUV entering the parking lot.

FIFTEEN

Felicity heard footsteps, then a loud knocking at the office door. A door she'd locked behind her when she came in this morning. She approached trying to ignore the feeling in her gut that it could be a murderer.

"Who is it?" she asked, trying for a confident tone.

"Felicity, it's me," Sam's answered.

She turned the lock and stepped back as he entered. He was holding two coffee cups on a cardboard tray in one hand, a brown paper carrier bag hanging from his fingers, leaving one hand free for knocking on doors, or grabbing his gun.

"I'm guessing you haven't eaten," he said and held up the bag.

"No, mostly because I was focused on what I was doing." Felicity felt a short wave of dizziness and realized how much time passed since she had eaten. "Amelie?"

"Bagels, cream cheese, lox and Americanos." He laid the food out on her desk. "Let's eat while we talk."

"Okay, but..." Felicity tried to keep the irritation out of her voice. She knew her hunger was making her impatient, but she needed to know about Amelie.

"But, nothing." He handed her a coffee. "I've got a call out about your friend, and I've asked the local force to keep an eye out for her. You starving won't help."

"Okay." She threw up her hands and conceded.

Sam layered salmon on the cream cheese he plastered on a poppy seed bagel. "It's getting harder to keep the investigation clean now the press has alerted everyone. We're gathering evidence while surrounded by crowds of tourists, not that they found out we have another body."

"I can't believe people are so morbid. At least the victims are found before it gets busy."

"Yep, it's like he plans it that way. He avoids the street cameras when he dumps the bodies. He finds places that fill quickly in the morning, and yet the bodies are found before the tourists get there. That's the only blessing here." He popped the lid on his coffee and took a long swallow.

"How will you catch him?" Felicity asked.

"We've been trying to look for a pattern, but no luck."

"No pattern at all?" She ripped a bagel half in pieces and placed a smear of cream cheese on one before popping it in her mouth.

"Not that we can see. There are similarities, yes, but no pattern we can find."

"I don't feel like going back to the files. Do you want to talk through it?" She rolled a slice of salmon around another chunk of bagel and sat back. "Maybe I can see something you're missing. You know that outsider's view. I am good with patterns."

Sam nodded. "Okay, if you feel up to it."

"I need to do something. Anything."

He put his coffee back on the table. "We have five bodies, two men three women."

"Yes." Felicity closed her eyes, trying to separate the people from the crimes. "And I may be connected to all of them."

"Uh huh," Sam said, before taking a bite of his bagel.

"And the victims are being left in prominent places. And we have some notes." Felicity pushed aside the remaining half of the bagel, no longer feeling like eating.

Sam swallowed. "Yes, the notes. So, we're missing two."

"Do we know what order they died?" She pushed aside the image of bodies that flashed into her mind.

Sam pulled his notebook out of his back pocket and checked what he had written. "Yes, I got that info today: David first then Brian, Agnes, Lila, and finally Katherine."

She nodded, before saying. "Okay, the men first. I'm not sure that's enough for a pattern but, it means David must have been held someplace. There's no way his body could have been there for any length of time. Too many people take the cable car. They would have noticed a body. Or a dog would have found him sooner."

"There was dust on his skin, like he'd been lying on the floor of a warehouse. Somewhere cold, there wasn't much deterioration." He put the book on her desk and sat back for a moment staring at the wall.

"What are you thinking about telling me?"

"There are some details we've kept back." He sat forward and lowered his voice as though to share a secret. "It's not easy stuff to hear."

"If it helps figure out who did it then I'll be able to hear it." Felicity hoped it was true.

"The bodies were mutilated." Sam picked up piece of paper from Felicity's desk, flipped it over to make sure both sides were blank, and then took his pen out of his pocket. "Here's what it looks like."

He drew three seven-pointed stars in the top left quarter of the paper. "The fairy star," Felicity breathed out the words.

Sam drew a stylized five-pointed flower in the bottom right. "A hidden pentacle," Felicity whispered.

In the top right, he quickly drew a circle topped by an upturned crescent, and in the bottom left a series of letters that looked like calligraphy.

"The Horned God." She pointed to the top right of the paper, then to the final drawing. "Runes, I don't know what they say. These are Wiccan symbols."

"There were burns that dripped. The pathologist thinks it's candle wax. There were dyes singed into the skin."

"It sounds like it was some kind of ritual," Felicity said, shaking her head. "Sam, this isn't Wicca, it's some kind of perversion of it. My beliefs are not about pain or torture. Look, The Rule of Three is part of our law; what ye send out comes back to thee times three. We don't hex. We don't curse. Bad energy comes back the same way as good energy. Three times as much as you send out."

"We did some research. We know it isn't really Wicca." Sam held up his hand as though to calm her down. "I don't know about Wicca but serial killers usually have some type of ritual they perform. Sometimes they pose the body. Sometimes they mutilate."

"So, the way these things are drawn on the body will be a clue?"

"Not drawn, the star was created by a sharp instrument puncturing the skin. The rest were carved into the skin. It was all done while the victim was alive."

Felicity felt the bagel in her stomach turn to a solid lump. The person who committed the crimes was violating the victim's bodies and spirits at the same time as they defiled her religion.

She touched the drawing. "I'll try to help but you have to tell me everything. I might see something you don't. You have done some research, but this is my belief, I'll see the nuances. He's perverting it, but there may be some things you'll miss. You can't hold back to protect me." She turned the drawing sideways. "I have to stop this person before more of my friends get hurt. Sam, you have got to find Amelie."

"We will. Focus on this while we wait."

She could feel her fears dissolve in the face of his confidence. "Okay, okay, were the bodies all the same?"

"No, the violence is escalating." He pulled a second sheet toward him. "That picture is what we found on Katherine's body. I'm sorry," he added when Felicity drew a sharp breath.

"Don't be. I keep trying to put the person out of my mind and think of it as an exercise. Like an art project. I'll pray their spirits find the Summerlands tonight." She wiped her eyes, tears were undermining her ability to see the clues, both physically and emotionally.

"Okay, if you're sure."

The symbols Sam first drew on the paper were similar to the others. Then he added more detail. The runes were cruder and malformed. The stars and pentacle were ragged and lopsided. Each section was circled in large dots.

"We think he was practicing on Katherine," he said. "The cuts are uneven. Like his knife wasn't sharp enough."

"What are the dots?" Felicity pointed to the drawing, not touching the paper. "I can't think of any significance."

"Burn marks," Sam said. "This isn't hesitant. He knows how to apply the instrument evenly. Each burn is the same level. It's made with something that maintained its heat for a while. Like a car lighter but smaller."

"I don't think this is a religious symbol. Do you know if he made the burns before the cuts?"

"No, but I can ask." Sam made a note. "Any reason you think it's a man?"

"I guess I just assumed based on the level of violence. Maybe I can't imagine that a woman could do that to someone. Sorry I guess that's just prejudice."

"It is, but you're right it does feel like a man is doing this. We can speculate, but there's not much we know right now." He counted out on his fingers. "One, the amount of damage done to the bodies is escalating based on the order they were killed. Two, there is a connection to you. Three, there's some kind of ritual being carried out and it's not likely to be finished yet. Four, all the bodies have been dumped in public places."

"Five," Felicity interrupted. "We know Amelie is still missing."

"Yes. I hope we find her, but the more time that passes the less likely it is we'll find her alive."

Felicity could feel fear flowing over her, slipping from her control. She had not missed having a family until now. She had no one to turn to. No one who would tell her it was all right, even when it wasn't.

"Lord and Lady protect her." Felicity looked at the piles of papers waiting to be re-filed then glanced at the drawing. Wiping tears away, she tucked her hair behind her ears, and pushed herself out of the chair. "If you don't have anything else to tell me, I think you'd be more useful out there investigating, and I'd be more useful at home doing some research on the signs and runes. I'm not going to let this maniac get away with this."

SIXTEEN

The next morning, Felicity hung up the phone as she heard Amelie's voicemail greeting start. Last night she worried about everyone she knew, trying to figure out who this person was, and why they were killing people. She had been calling Amelie's number almost hourly since three am. Still no contact from her friend and she knew it was likely that Amelie was in trouble, but every time Felicity's mind said, 'she's gone' her heart replied, 'keep hoping'.

She returned to sit on the couch where Sam's drawings lay on the coffee table beside four books of Wiccan knowledge and her laptop. She had been searching everything she could think of to make sense of the symbols. She'd found each one. She knew them well as symbols of her religion, but each held other meanings. She could not find any reference to the symbols as they related to this kind of ritual. She even checked Satanic rites with no luck.

Footsteps on the stairs outside her home broke her train of thought. She recognized Sam's energetic step and went to the door but waited for him to identify himself.

"Have you heard from anyone about Amelie?" she asked relief and fear battling for control of her emotions.

"Sorry." Sam shook his head. "Not yet. Why don't you sit down?"

Felicity sat, fist clenched, waiting for the bad news. Sam would not have told her to sit unless it was bad news.

"We've found another body." He reached out and touched her shoulder. "It's not Amelie, it's a man."

"I guess that means you don't know who it is, right?" She put her hand over his and kept it there, feeling comforted by the contact.

"That's right."

"Do you need me to identify him?" She swallowed the dread that rose with the thought of looking at a victim.

"No. We're trying for dental records or fingerprints. There's a lot of damage, and I don't know if anyone except his mother, or wife if he has one, could tell us who he was by looking at the body."

"I guess the body has the same cuts and burns. Is that why you came? It's part of the pattern?"

"Yes, and it's getting worse."

"How?"

"No. You don't want to know the details."

"I know you are trying to protect me, but that's not right. If I can do anything, even lose a few nights to evil dreams, then I will." She let go of his hand and stood, anger flooding her, driving out the fear and horror. "These are my friends. If you protect me at the cost of their lives, it won't be worth it to me, or to their families. There may be a chance for us to save Amelie."

"No, it's not that easy. You need to know something before we go any further. You have to understand that this won't be just a few nightmares. It could be years of dealing with the fallout of what you see."

"I have my faith." He seemed about to hug her. Felicity stepped back, unwilling to take comfort until he told her.

"Faith doesn't always help," he said.

"And sometimes it does." She went to the closet and pulled out her coat. "I assume you don't have pictures."

"No. Not with me."

"I know you don't think I can handle it, but at this point I can handle anything that will help stop this guy." She picked up her house keys from the table by the front door. "You drive."

SUNDAY AFTERNOON DRIVING in San Francisco was slow and required a lot of patience. The tourists would not have been an obstacle if the city was flat and the streets were straight. Of course, it is unlikely that there would be tourists without the hills and curves.

"This body was found at Candlestick Park," Sam said.

Felicity turned to face him. "Is it a baseball player? I don't know any."

"No, but there are cameras all around the parking lot. We thought we would catch a break."

"But you didn't?"

"No, all we saw was someone walk across the lot and roll the body out of some kind of heavy plastic sheeting."

"You couldn't see anything to identify him?"

"No, not really enough to confirm that it was a him. We assume it was. The body would have been too heavy for most women to carry. But the killer was wearing bulky clothing, and their jacket hood was pulled up."

Felicity turned back to watching the crowded streets slide by. She tried not to think about how impossible it seemed that they were going to stop the killing, or what she was about to do.

The pictures had been bad enough, she dreaded the thought of seeing the damage on this victim's body.

"You don't have to do this," Sam said as he pulled into the parking lot. "We can wait for the fingerprints or dental search to come back."

"I think I should see the body and the damage in reality. It might make some kind of sense of the symbols that I'm not getting from your drawings." Her voice was low, and she forced her breath in and out.

"The morgue is down in the basement." Sam waited for her to enter the elevator and then pushed the button labeled B.

She followed him down the hall to the room at the far end where she knew the body waited. Her stomach was doing warm up exercises in anticipation of the sight of the body. She tried to keep her breathing long and slow, but it seemed her lungs could not pull in enough air. She was on the edge of gasping each time she drew in a breath.

When the police officers showed her the pictures of the first body, she'd had no time for anticipation, or rather dread, just a shock as she looked at the photo. The buildup of emotion as she approached the window almost made her bolt. The knowledge that this might save her best friend, kept her feet moving forward.

Sam's hand on her elbow checked her progress. "We're here, Felicity. Are you going to be okay with this?"

"No, but let's get it over with." She tried not to lean on Sam. She needed to do this herself.

"Look through here." He pointed to the window, the blinds were down, but the slats were open. She looked through the spaces between the thin slats at a metal gurney. A body lay there under a white sheet.

Sam pressed a button on the right side of the window. "Okay, show us, please."

Felicity noticed the woman in the white coat standing quietly to the side of the gurney. The woman reached for the sheet at the top of the covered body and carefully exposed only the head.

"Blessed be, the poor man." Felicity felt tears rise at the sight of the pale features.

"Do you know him?" Sam moved closer, his presence warming her.

"I think I do. Can you tell me if he's missing his right thumb?" she asked quietly.

Sam relayed the request. The woman nodded then walked around the gurney to lift the sheet enough to pull out the body's hand. The thumb was missing. The wound old and healed in hard folds of skin around a short stub.

"His name is Finn Walker. He runs TempExperts we have a friendly rivalry. I mean we had one." Her energy drained, leaving her cold and exhausted. "I can't do this anymore. Can we go?"

Sam thanked the woman behind the glass and put his arm around Felicity, drawing her into his shoulder. "Yes, come on. I'll take you home."

"Can you tell me anything about this murder?" Felicity asked, desperately hoping that the details would help her stop the killer.

"When I get you home and I've called in his ID. Someone needs to tell his family."

"He doesn't have one." The tears slid over her lashes and fell down her cheeks. "His family was in New York visiting the twin towers on September eleventh. He buried them in the grave-yard, and then himself in his work."

SEVENTEEN

The warehouse was silent. Other buildings in the area were full of workers going about their business. On his way to the grey door that led into his building, Sid passed forklifts whisking in and out of the back of parked semis, and workers lounging in overalls, on their last smoke break of the day. Sid liked this time of day. He felt a residual energy come from the bustle of the ordinary lives around him. He smiled at the thought of how he would pull the energy into his ritual.

Standing in the middle of the floor with all the lights on, Sid listened to the buzz of the fluorescent tubes as they warmed up. It was important to make sure there was no evidence left of the last ritual. He did not want to sully this new ceremony with the energy of the old one. He did not want to mix the gender pain that might linger in some trace of blood or urine from the woman. The new ritual wouldn't be carried out for a couple of days but needed a lot of planning. Sid frowned. He had not yet gathered enough knowledge about this person to know when to take him, or where to dump the body.

Sid sniffed the air. There was no trace of blood. He decided to clean the floor again and use the mindless actions to center his thoughts. In a small closet in the back of his storage area, there was a large jug of bleach, a mop, and a wringer pail. He poured a quart of bleach into the bucket and took it to the bathroom to add water.

He hummed as he walked to the center of the room and poured the watery bleach out in one flood, spinning as he did to create a wide wet circle. The water drifted toward a drain at the bottom of a depression in the floor near the front door.

Sid's humming was tuneless and rhythmic as he used a stiff broom to scrape the water toward the drain. In his mind, he felt a hush blossom, damping all input including the sharp clean smell of the bleach. He smiled as his focus slipped away from the movement of his body. His body continued its routine sweeping with no input from Sid's mind.

"Rosemary for remembrance, and lemon for focus," he muttered. "Blood-red candles and white feathers. That will be the air sacrifice."

He continued to sweep the last pools of bleach toward the drain. Looking at the floor, he saw one stain. It was a splash of dark on the floor, just to the left of where the sacrifice's head had been. He pulled the bucket with him as he moved closer to inspect it. Blood would be gone with the bleach. Sid hesitated before leaning down and touching the stain with his finger. It left a smudge on the tip. He brought the finger to his nose and sniffed, oil and ashes. Walking back to the closet, Sid pulled a bottle of dishwashing liquid from a shelf. He squirted it onto the stain and started scrubbing.

"I'll dedicate the blood to the spirit of water. Fire is easy, but I'll need a new box of matches to burn the flesh." Sid added the items to his mental list as he spoke. "Earth, now I'll need something special for earth. Not sand, too hard to clean completely. Not dust, too common. Not ashes, don't want to have another sticky stain."

When the last of the water drained away, Sid put the broom over his shoulder, picked up the empty bucket, and walked back to replace the equipment, his cleaning finished. He moved around, opening bags and plastic containers looking for inspiration in the contents.

"Perfect," he said as he opened a two-ply brown paper bag. "Flour, the man works with it enough. And some soil from the planter in Her front yard."

His ingredients identified, Sid moved on to the details of the ritual, his tools, and process. He shuffled over to the altar table in the back of the room and uncovered the knife in the black cloth. He tested it against his fingertip and shook his head at the dullness of the edge. He pulled a square of fine grey stone from a drawer and started sharpening the knife. He'd learned that sharp knives cut better symbols. He started humming again in counterpoint to the whine of the metal on the whetstone. He needed a message for Felicity. Something she would understand. Something to praise her. Something to please her.

EIGHTEEN

It had been two days since Felicity identified Finn. Two days that she spent wandering through her routine. Bone deep tiredness left her listless. She performed the passing rite for Finn and any unknown souls who had fallen victim to the killer. The ceremony left her empty, but not with the feeling of peace she normally felt in the presence of the Lady.

There was still no news about Amelie. Felicity had given up hope, and simply waited for the call that she knew would eventually come.

She lay on her sofa and stared at the white ceiling, trying to sleep with no luck. "Get up and do something," she said, raising herself up. Lying there was just making her feel less alive. Pushing her sleeves up and her hair behind her ears, she looked around her small living room. It was untidy and shabby in the warm fall sunlight that came through the window. She went into the cleaning cupboard and grabbed a handful of rags and the natural spray polish that she used to shine her furniture.

She surveyed the room. The first step was to put all the items from the coffee table onto the chair so she could clean the surface. The TV remote and the novel she had been reading went onto the red fabric of the seat. The glass of water and its coaster went on the floor. The coaster on top to keep the excess spray out of the glass. The pens and notepaper that were there from a session of frantic note taking in the wee hours of the morning ended up on the couch.

When the table was clear, she sprayed the orange oil onto the top and wiped the dust with a rag. As she wiped, the cloth caught on something on the edge of table, leaning in for a better look, she saw a dark red mess spread down the wood. Her breath stopped and chills flooded her. *Stop being a wimp*, Felicity thought.

She reached over, cloth in hand and carefully scratched it up. It was sticky. She brought it closer and sniffed: ketchup. Her muscles relaxed and Felicity chuckled. She gave a final buff to the table and saw the wood surface glow.

The hardwood floors took only a dry duster and five minutes. When she was finished, Felicity felt as though the exercise had done its job. She put the cleaning items away and decided to organize her kitchen cupboards. Her energy was returning with the simple work.

Placing the contents of the spice cupboard on the table, she started checking each one to see if they were still usable. Those that smelled off, or did not have any scent, went in the garbage and those that were still good went back in the cupboard in alphabetical order. She checked the canned goods, none showed expired 'best before' dates. Her fridge was empty except for a jug of water and some condiments.

Felicity's worry and stress lifted as she achieved glowing cleanliness in her home. "Time to get some food in the house I think." She took her coat off the hook. Deciding to make a grocery list tomorrow and re-stock the basics then, she swore that tonight was the last time she would pick up dinner and eat in the office. The files she had been reviewing almost a week ago still needed finishing, and when that was done, she was determined there would be no more late nights at the office.

STANDING IN HER OFFICE, Felicity looked at the backlog of files. She wanted to bring the same sense of order here as she felt in her home. If she could keep order in her own spaces, maybe order would come to the world around her. She looked the files over again and realized that she could probably fill two storage boxes with old files as she culled. Her business was growing faster than she could keep up. It was definitely time to let Isaac hire a part time helper.

Putting the sandwich and soda on her desk, she went to the storeroom for the flat pack cardboard. She folded and tucked the cardboard until she had two sturdy crates with lids attached. Then she took the first pile of six files and started to sort through them.

In the back of the O'Bannon file, she found a sheet of stiff parchment. At first glance, the writing was familiar, but she couldn't place it.

A FRIEND IS NOT *a friend who turns his back. He turned from you and now he has paid.*

You trusted him with a secret and he told a stranger.

Lord and Lady turn your backs. He hurt your aspect on Earth

THE PEACE and contentment that came with the homey activities slid away, leaving behind a damp cold sickness that threatened to drown her. The killer had been back in her office.

There was no chance the police missed this note when they searched last week.

She grabbed the phone off her desk and dialed the number Sam had given her. When he answered, she told him about the letter hearing her voice tremble. He told her to stay in her office and lock the door. He was on his way.

While she waited, Felicity knew she needed to keep busy or she would go crazy. She walked over to the filing cabinet and started shaking open folders from the pile on top. Five files showered their contents to the floor without revealing a new sheet of stiff cream-colored paper. She shook the sixth file and a note skittered across the paper avalanche. The tenth file produced two notes; the twelfth file one more and the final file produced one more.

"Felicity, open the door."

The sound of Sam's voice broke through her panic. She ran to the door and threw herself at him. "I found more notes, Sam I found six more notes, that's nine bodies. Nine people who died because of me." She gasped out the words, tears sliding down her cheeks.

"No. Not because of you." He wrapped his arms around her. "They are dead because some maniac is killing people. Never think it has anything to do with you."

In his arms, the panic building in her body since she found the first note started to recede. Her tears slowed to a stop. Sam hugged her a little closer as she sighed out the last of the emotions.

"Okay," he said as she drew away. "Let's go in the kitchen. I'll call the crime scene team."

AN HOUR and a half hour later, Felicity stood in the doorway to her office and watched the forensic team pack up their tools in preparation to leave. They'd come to the door ten minutes after Sam called them. Since entering, the four men in full plastic suits had dusted every surface, pried into every drawer, and shone lights in every corner of the office.

While Sam showed them out, Felicity picked up a handful of the scattered papers and placed them on the desk. She was hollow. There were no feelings, no tears, no outrage.

Sam touched her shoulder and turned her to face him. "You need to get away from this. I'll take you home and you can pack a bag. Let's check you into a hotel for the night. We can figure out the best way to deal with this in the morning."

"No," she spat the word, trying to stoke her anger again. It felt like the only way she could keep her terror at bay. Felicity turned away and bent for more papers, unable to stop tidying the mess. "I will not let this maniac push me out of my life. I don't want to cower in a hotel room. I need to be able to sleep in my own bed. We need to find this guy and put him away."

"I don't like it. I want you safe." Sam hesitated. Felicity thought he was about to order her to stay in a hotel. Then he sighed. "I can put some people outside to watch your place. It will be harder than keeping you safe in a hotel, but I understand what you mean. Felicity, if it makes you feel better, I don't think he's trying to hurt you. All his notes say he's doing this for you."

"Oh, great. Yes, that makes me feel so much better." Felicity took her coat from where it was hanging on her doorknob. "I need to get some cleaning supplies. Your forensic team has left powder and stuff all over this place."

Sam took her coat and held it for her to slide her arms in. "No, don't worry about that. We'll send a cleaning team. You're in shock. You just need to go home and rest."

Felicity felt the heat of tears pushing from behind her eyes. She couldn't stop herself being stubborn about this. The man who was killing all her friends was getting away with it. How would they catch him if he could ghost in and out of her office?

"How can I rest?" she snapped. "I don't know if I have any friends left. Every time I get someone's voicemail, I imagine them dead, and mutilated."

Sam picked up the evidence bags that contained the notes. "I get it. Look, it'll take a while for them to find a team to sit outside your house. Come with me while I check these in, then I'll wait with you until I know you are safe."

"I'm sorry. I know you are doing everything you can. I know you're trying to protect me. I'll try not to make it harder." Felicity felt her heart slow and her temper fade. "Could we get copies of the notes? Maybe we can try to make some sense, or order, of them while we wait. I'm not going to be able to sleep, I might as well work."

NINETEEN

"Tea?" Felicity asked as she held out her hand for Sam's jacket when they were back in her house. She saw his gun harness as he shrugged off his jacket. She normally did not like guns, but tonight it made her feel safe. "Or I can make coffee if you like."

"Coffee would be great."

Felicity turned the kettle on to make tea for herself and put coffee in the drip pot for Sam. She could see him setting up in the living room. Pulling out the copies of the notes, he laid them side by side on the coffee table. She poured milk into a jug, sugar into a bowl, and placed them with two mugs on a tray. When the tea and coffee were ready, she took the tray into the living room and placed it on the end of the coffee table.

She nodded at the notes, a shiver of dread threading its way into her heart. "When you lay them out like that, it seems so many. I don't know where to start."

Sam grunted. "It looks like there are more bodies out there than we thought. If we can identify as many of the notes as possible, then maybe we'll have an idea where to start looking for this guy."

Felicity's shoulders slumped. "I look at this and see bodies of friends, people who have been tortured. I don't know how to get past that."

"You need to stop thinking of them as people. I know that sounds cold, but if you don't then we won't be able to see the facts and patterns." Sam patted the couch beside him. "Felicity, try to put their lives in the background. These are clues to catching this crazy man."

"I'll try." She closed her eyes and pushed the images of death aside. Nodding to the nine notes on the table, she asked, "Where do we start?"

"Let's separate them into two piles, male and female." His tone was matter of fact.

"Okay, there are notes for four men and five women." She tidied the edges of each pile.

"Where do you want to start?" Sam asked.

"Men." Felicity thought the shortest list would be fastest, and by then, maybe she would have found some detachment.

Sam read the note on the top of the pile. "*A friend is not a friend who turns his back. He turned from you and now he has paid. You trusted him with a secret and he told a stranger.*"

"I think that's David. I told him I was going to break up with my then boyfriend in confidence and he told the boyfriend. The break up didn't go as easy as I hoped it would." Felicity shook her head. "That was years ago. Do you think this has been in the works that long?"

Sam wrote David's name on the copy of the note and put the paper to the side. "Not likely, these guys aren't the most patient people I know. He may have picked David because you were friends, and then got the information during the process."

"During the process, is that how you distance yourself?" Felicity tried not to snap. She realized Sam was doing everything he could to help. It just felt so inhuman.

"Yes," Sam answered and picked up the next note. "*He was*

not willing to stay a rival. He planned to destroy your livelihood. Now he is the one destroyed.'" He looked expectantly at Felicity.

"Finn," she said. "It was a friendly rivalry. There's enough temp work in this city to support another ten companies. No one in our business needs to be that cutthroat."

Sam put Finn's name on the paper and placed it on top of David's.

Felicity picked the next note from the pile. *"'He touched you roughly and made no excuse. Now he pays tribute with his soul. No one who abuses you will pass through the portals to the Summerland.'"*

"Any idea who that could be?" Sam asked.

"No idea. No one has manhandled me or pushed me around."

"Okay, we'll put that on the pile for unknown." Sam picked up the last note. *"'This one wanted help but when he saw your name, he said he would not take aid from a woman. Now he won't be hiring anyone ever again. Lord and Lady turn your backs, he slighted your aspect on earth.'* This isn't exactly Shakespeare."

"I know, it's awful. I think that must be Brian Wells." Felicity felt herself becoming more businesslike as they worked through the list. Sam was right, a bit of distance helped her think clearly. "Remember, he had my business card on him when they found him."

"Okay," Sam said, writing Brian's name on the sheet and putting it on the known pile. "That means we need to identify which notes refer to Agnes, Lila, and Katherine."

"Katherine is probably the note about failing a trial. I think he means that I knew that the client would be inappropriate, and I expected Katherine to put up with it."

"Makes sense." Sam wrote Katherine's name on the note and started a pile for women.

"I think the one about retail is the sales clerk in the shoe store." Felicity looked up. "Did you find out about her?"

"No body, but she's missing. Her name was Vera." Sam wrote a question mark after her name and added the note to the identified list.

"Wasn't Lila's last name Rose?" Felicity asked, picking up a note.

"Yes."

"This is probably about her. '*By any other name would this rose would be treacherous. She took credit for lovely Amanda's idea and got a promotion. Amanda won't be called back and so you lost a client.*'" Felicity handed Sam the note. "You know, a rose by any other name."

"Two notes left, '*She tried to tear your treasure away. The Lord and Lady prevented it. Now she rests in the pit*'. Could this be Agnes?"

"I don't know." Felicity took a sip of tea to give herself time to think. "Someone tried to steal my purse a few weeks ago. Do you think that might be about her? I'm sure it wasn't Agnes Thomas. You said she was older, right? The would-be thief was in her twenties."

"Okay, we'll put that note on the pile of unknowns right now." Sam wrote purse-snatcher on the note before depositing it on the pile.

Felicity picked up the last note, "'*A harridan reaps the fruit of her harvest. She made her husband close the account. You tried to help him and she turned your kindness to base use.*'"

"Does it ring any bells?"

"No, I suppose it could be Agnes, but I can't be sure until I know who Agnes is."

"So, three notes in the unidentified pile, one body with no note confirmed." Sam folded the papers in half in their separate piles and started to put them in his jacket pocket. His phone rang as he completed the task.

"Yes." He listened to the person on the other side. "Okay, I'll be leaving in a few minutes."

"Is there news?"

"No. The protection team is here. I'll call you as soon as I have anything. Try to get some sleep."

"I'm sorry we didn't make any breakthroughs," Felicity said.

"Don't worry about it. At least we have some new information. You identifying the notes and the bodies will be of use to a profiler or analyst. They might be able to give us more potential characteristics. Something that might trigger your memory."

Felicity walked him to the door and locked it. She cleaned up the tea and coffee dishes and went to bed. She wasn't optimistic that she would be able to sleep, but lying down would, at least, give her some rest.

TWENTY

The sound of the phone broke through her doze and Felicity grabbed the receiver before the second ring finished.

"Yes?" She felt her heart thud with the shock of waking.

"Felicity, sorry to wake you, but I have some news. I thought you would like to hear it as soon as possible." She could hear the strain in Sam's voice. He had gone back to work, then. Felicity wondered if he was sleeping any more than she was.

"It's okay. I wasn't really sleeping. Is it about Amelie?"

"No, it's Agnes." Sam paused, and she could hear paper rustling. "You didn't recognize her because she went back to her maiden name after a divorce. Do you recognize the name Agnes Adamson?"

"Oh, yes." She rubbed the sleep from her eyes. "She divorced a client of mine, Craig Adamson. I should have thought of her, but he always called her Aggie. She was a real barracuda. When she was done, he had to close down his business. So, I guess, she was the harridan after all."

"Yep." Sam hesitated. "I'm sorry. That could have waited, I didn't think."

"No, don't be sorry. But..."

"What?"

"Have you been able to find anything out about Amelie?"

"I'm sorry, no. She is still missing. Don't give up hope. I'm told her job can take her off the grid for a while."

"Not without letting me know she can't make it. Even if she couldn't tell me why. Sam, I'm afraid she's the next body." Tears started to form again. She swallowed and wiped her eyes.

"I don't think you should give up hope. We're doing everything we can to find her."

Felicity said goodbye and flopped back down on the bed. All chance of sleep gone. She checked the time on her alarm clock, four am. The constant fear that invaded her life since the day the two policemen came to her office, had become familiar, and lost its power to do anything more than drain her energy.

Getting up she went to her study to do some research on the notes. After searching online and reading hundreds of links and blog entries to find any reference to a Wiccan path that would support the killer's belief, she started an email to Sam giving him information that may help determine how the notes related to Wicca.

There are many paths to follow in Wiccan belief, but these notes don't make sense to any path I know. He signs off the notes with an error when he refers to an aspect of the Lord and Lady on Earth. There is no such concept. We believe that the Lord and Lady are aspects of the All. The All is represented in different faces by aspects of youth, adult, and age. I don't know if he's trying to refer to one of the aspects of the Lady: child, woman, and hag. The closest we come to having an earthly aspect is that certain ceremonies seem to fill the priest/priestess with the aspect they are invoking.

There is no devil, heaven, or hell in our belief. The references to Satan's table, eternal trials, devils, have no place in Wicca. The two laws of Wicca are; if you aren't hurting anyone, do what you will, and what you send out will come back threefold. The second law is what generally keeps Wiccans from throwing curses around and being bullies. No one will act to hurt anyone if they know the pain will come to them three times over.

Not much help and nothing new, she thought, but at least it should give them some idea of how far he's gone away from Wicca.

After completing the information and sending it to the email address on Sam's card, she checked through the window to see where the protection team was. She saw the black sedan parked across the intersection; two shapes seemed to be watching her.

Her research had taken almost two hours and hadn't made her any sleepier. She decided to make breakfast for the two men in the car before going to work.

TWENTY-ONE

Lulu drove her courier van through the dark streets. This was her favorite time of day. Too early for the rush of people going to work, but late enough that the city seemed to be holding its breath anticipating the coming day. It was a couple of hours before the glow of predawn, but the street lights cast enough light to show the few people already on the streets.

She liked the contrasts of white, grey, and black that happened at this time. She worked this early shift so she could spend the noisy hours in her studio. Lulu's paintings were textures of light against a background of night black. Her favorite work was the street scene after a fight. A pool of scarlet blood at the edge of a white sheet of light from the lamps, the slab of the building looming behind.

The open plaza in front of the civic center inspired her because the textures of the brick and stone pavers picked out in the stark glare of her headlights, and the shadows of the trees striped the open area with black. This morning, a pale shape in the center of the open space seemed to have risen from a sea made of stone.

Lulu looked closer. The shape was folded and twisted into a

pile. There was something compelling about it. She stopped the truck and locked the doors, so no one could slip in and lift any of the documents she still needed to deliver.

Walking across the plaza, Lulu tried to figure out what was so familiar about the shape. As her mind recognized the fingers and arms of a human being, her stomach rebelled. She ran to a far corner of the plaza pulling her phone from her jeans. She retched up her breakfast into a garbage container and then dialed 911.

"Ambulance and Police," she rasped. "United Nations plaza, there's a body. Yes, I can wait for them, no I haven't touched anything."

Ten minutes later, Lulu saw the flashing lights of the police cars, and the plaza started to fill with official activity.

"Can you tell me what you saw?" the man who had identified himself as Special Agent Sam Barton asked.

"All I saw was the body. I didn't recognize it as a body at first, only when I got close enough." She shuddered. "I didn't think a person could be folded up that way. Jesus Christ, he must have broken every major joint in her body."

"Why do you say he?" Sam asked.

"That must have taken a lot of strength. I used to do martial arts and I know how much damage you can inflict, or rather get inflicted on you, and how much strength it takes to break something. That was a man, or a freakishly strong woman."

"Are you usually down here at this time of the morning?"

"Yes. I deliver documents to the government offices. They like to get things done early in the day." Lulu checked her watch. "I need to get going soon if I'm going to make my rounds on time."

"Just one more question. Is there anything, other than the body, different this morning?"

"No. Same as always, just me and the truck until I head

back. By then the first few early risers start showing up." She nodded toward the cameras facing the square. "They should give you the whole picture."

"Thanks. If anything else comes to mind call me." Sam handed Lulu his card, and she provided her contact information, proving her address with her driver's license.

TWENTY-TWO

The agents outside Felicity's home gratefully accepted the coffee and muffins she offered for breakfast. She felt safer with them inside her house while she showered and prepared for work. They drove her to the office, and told her to let Sam know when she planned to go home, so he could get them in place for tomorrow night if necessary.

The door was unlocked when she arrived. Felicity paused on the top step. The police kept a set of keys so she was expecting to find it locked. She opened the door carefully prepared to run if anyone threatened her. The cleaning team had already removed all traces of the scene investigation team's work. The papers were now in a box in Felicity's office. She wasn't looking forward to going through it and reorganizing the papers again.

"Hey, boss." Isaac's cheerful voice greeted her. "What happened last night? I got here and there was a crew cleaning up. A rather cute cleaning crew at that. They told me there had been a crime. I tell you they made me show identification and pass the third degree just to get to my own desk."

"Morning, Isaac. Yes, there was an investigation. I don't know if I'm allowed to pass on the details but it means we have a lot of filing to do. Sorry." Felicity wasn't willing to feed Isaac's appetite for gossip.

"No, we *had* a lot of filing to do. I'm almost done." He pointed to a box on the floor by his desk. It contained hanging files each labeled with the client name. There was a pile of papers an inch high on his desk. "I've packed up the closed ones, these are active. Give me five more minutes and I can put them back in the cabinet."

"What would I do without you?"

"Obviously, you would drown in paperwork." He laughed. "When I took a week off last month, I didn't realize how behind it would get."

"And all the investigation hasn't helped. Every time we clean up, it gets all tossed around again. You can add part time office assistant to the list of positions we are hiring for. I don't want you to have to do filing all the time. I think you should start taking more responsibility." She grabbed him in a hug and kissed him on the cheek before going into her office.

Without the filing, she wasn't sure what to do. Normally her workload exceeded her capacity and it was sometimes exhausting, but always exhilarating. Today she couldn't find a place to start.

As promised, Isaac came into her office with the box and quickly placed the active files in the right drawers. "You look like crap, sweetie. I mean that in the nicest way possible. Are you sleeping?"

"Not really. There's a lot of stuff happening, and I'm not getting my eight hours. Not even three, truth be told."

"You should make an appointment for a spa treatment. That always perks me up," Isaac suggested.

"Maybe another time. What's on the plate today?"

"There are four new client applications to process, and we've got three contracts ending next week. And there are six applicants for the job you put in the paper."

"Okay, why don't you do the credit and Better Business checks on the new clients. I'll look at the job applications. We can put our heads together on who to interview." Felicity held out her hand for the sheaf of resumes, glad for some normal activity to keep her mind active. "We'll go over the schedule this afternoon. I'll treat us to lunch. How does that sound?"

"Excellent executive decisions." Isaac smiled. "There, you look better already. You just needed something to work on. I'll make reservations for lunch. Italian?"

"Perfect."

When she was alone Felicity realized she didn't want to pick through the resumes. She needed to find Amelie. This time when she called Amelie's employer she asked to speak to a partner in the detective agency.

"Yes, Ms. Armstrong. My name is Jackson Ingleton." The voice was brisk and professional.

"I'm trying to find Ms. Singh. Can you tell me if you know where she is?" Felicity knew that an outright question would only gain her the official party line of no information, but she couldn't think of a smoother way to approach it.

"I can't tell you where she is." Mr. Ingleton hesitated. "Are you the person who called last week?"

"Yes, she was supposed to meet me for dinner and I haven't heard from her. I know she can be on assignment for days, but this seems too long."

"We haven't seen Amelie since the morning you called." The voice warmed from the official chill. "We have filed a missing person's report."

"Did the FBI contact you?" Felicity wondered why Sam had not found out what was going on.

"Someone spoke to my partner. I am afraid we couldn't give them any information."

"Thank you. I'll follow up with the police." Well, with the FBI, she thought.

"Please let us know if we can help. We are very worried about her." His voice warmed even more. "I'm very worried about her."

"I'll let you know as soon as I hear anything. Will you do the same for me?"

"If we can. But if it has anything to do with a client, we won't be able to violate the confidentiality," Ingleton admitted.

"I understand." Felicity hoped that their client wasn't the killer. Mr. Ingleton didn't sound like the kind of man who liked to have anyone question his clients. She provided her contact information and hung up.

"Handsome Sam is here to see you," Isaac said sotto voce as he opened the door.

"Hey, I can hear you," Sam called back.

"Well, I didn't say anything mean." Isaac winked. "Go on through," he added as Felicity beckoned Sam into her office.

She rose. "I just spoke to Amelie's boss."

"Felicity, sit down." Sam pointed to her chair, his face serious.

She sat. "What? Just tell me Sam."

"It's Amelie," Sam said. "She was found in the United Nations Plaza outside the Civic Center, this morning."

"How do you know it's her?"

"There was a missing person's report. It gave a very detailed description. She had a tattoo on her right hip that was still visible. The cops are calling her boss right now. Let him identify her." Sam held up his hand as Felicity opened her mouth to speak. "It's bad. It makes Finn look like he died in his sleep. I don't want you to see it. I'm sorry, Felicity."

Felicity waited for the emotion. Nothing came, she felt empty. "It's not your fault. I guess it's not a surprise. It feels like I've known all along. What should we do now?"

"You need to go home. I'll get the team ready to cover your place." He reached for her desk phone.

"No. I won't sit at home and worry about what's going on. I need to do something, even if it's just work." She put her hand on his.

"No. I need you to be safe."

"You said he's not after me."

He stepped closer. "I'm not sure, that's true anymore."

"You aren't sure it's not. Sam, I will go crazy if I have to sit and wait for you to tell me about the next body."

He seemed about to argue but shook his head and took her hands. "Okay, I can understand that. That email you sent was a good idea. If we get together and talk this through we might figure something out."

"Like a brainstorming session?" She could hear the doubt in her own voice.

"Yes, it's worked before. It helps to get everyone on the same page, with the same information. And it brings assumptions into the light. Like your email, I didn't even question that there was anything wrong with the Wicca stuff. There may be things about the case we don't know enough about to question."

Felicity decided to trust Sam's knowledge. "I'll do whatever you think will help."

"I'll call Morton and Kang to set it up. There's also a behavioral analyst working with me, I'll call her in." He squeezed her hands. She could see the concern in his eyes. "Are you sure you don't need some time? I thought you'd be more upset about Amelie."

"I am. I just can't seem to feel anything." Felicity shrugged. "It feels like someone has wrapped me in damp wool. I'm cold all the time, and everything is muffled. I need to be doing something, anything, to help stop this man."

Sam shook his head. "It's pretty common to feel that way. Some people have a delayed reaction. We'll keep working through this."

TWENTY-THREE

The conference room in the police station was small. Five people made it feel crowded. The walls were covered in sheets of flipchart paper, most of which were covered in notes and diagrams. Morton and Kang sat at the table with Felicity. Sam leaned against the one wall of windows. Esther Greene, the behavioral analyst was picking through the pens on the table.

"We have two sites with cameras. The first one, we don't see enough detail to identify anyone. The second one, all we see is the body roll into camera range," Bobby Morton said at the end of his summary of the murders.

"Is there anything else we should be looking at?" Kang looked at Felicity as he asked the question that up until now had elicited one more question, idea, or answer.

"I don't know." She tried to keep her tone neutral, but Kang had been sniping at her for the last two hours and she heard the frustration leaking through.

Esther pointed to the sheet that contained the information on Wicca. "One thing we haven't talked about is how many more there might be."

"It's hard to say where he's getting his knowledge from,"

Sam offered. "Felicity, didn't you say that thirteen is some important number."

"Yes. If he's following that, then we're looking for five more bodies, and probably in the next nine days," Felicity confirmed. "We know from the notes that there are two women and one man out there somewhere that we haven't found yet."

"Do you think the gender is important?" Esther asked.

"Maybe to him, but not a reason that is legitimate to the faith," Felicity answered.

Kang threw his paper coffee cup into the trash can. "It's convenient that you don't know the significance of any of the religious aspects of the crimes."

"What do you mean by that?" Felicity snapped back at him. "He's a maniac, and he's using my religion to justify his twisted behavior."

"I just think you must know something that you aren't telling us," Kang said.

Her anger flooded out through the hold she usually managed to keep on her temper. "Because I should understand his behavior? We all seem to agree he's a man, what are you not telling us. As a man, you should know what he's doing."

"No one is saying you're hiding anything." Sam walked over to stand behind Felicity. "Detective Kang is trying to solve this with us."

"I don't think we should be focusing on the religion in particular," Esther said. "If we look at his words then we can see he has made this up out of whole cloth. His references are to Christian beliefs as well as to Wicca. I think he's been instructed in both, but it's gotten all twisted up in his obsession."

Felicity decided to ask the question that had been nagging at her since this started, "Why would he have picked me? What is it about me that would inspire him to do this?"

"It's hard to say." Esther doodled on a scrap of paper. "If he has a religious fixation, it might be that you resemble his idea of a goddess. His notes seem to support that. If he is fixated on something physical, it could be you fit a type, and he's just over-laid the religious stuff. Whatever it is, you probably didn't even notice him the first time he saw you. And you've seen him several times without knowing it. He's close to you, and he will be drawn to contact you."

"Lord and Lady, give me the strength to deal with this," Felicity whispered. "Will I know when he tries to contact me?"

"Unlikely. Until he's finished whatever ritual he's living out, you won't know who he is."

"Okay," Bobby Morton chipped in. "What do you suggest we focus on before the next mutilation happens?"

Esther turned to answer. "I think the only thing the religion references tell us is that he has come to relate death with belief. This is not uncommon in fanatical behavior. Think of Jim Jones, or Heaven's gate. The concept that in order to achieve some goal one must escape the earthly body is not new. What is inter-esting in this case is that there is so much detail involved. The mutilations are specific, and highly precise. That takes time and patience."

"Okay, so, we know he needs space to do this stuff and he needs a place where no one is going to hear the victims." Morton sighed. "This is just going around in circles again. We have a lot of information that isn't giving us leads."

"That's right." Kang leaned forward in his chair and looked at Felicity over the empty pizza boxes. "The only concrete thing we have is that all the victims are connected to you."

"Are you saying I did this? Why would I?" Ashamed of her reaction, Felicity clamped down on her temper and tried to follow Kang's reasoning. Perhaps if she did, then he would give up and focus on finding who was doing this rather than trying to pin it on her.

"Yes. What's the motive?" Sam asked.

"Money?"

Felicity shrugged. "What money? I don't have a lot of money hidden away."

"We've investigated that, and she's telling the truth." Sam looked at Felicity. "Sorry, it was part of eliminating you as a suspect."

Felicity frowned. "Why do you know that, and the police don't?"

"Normally, they wouldn't be part of the investigation. We're not used to cooperating, so I guess we haven't shared all our information." Sam shrugged. "I'll make sure that changes."

"What about that house. You own the whole thing. It's got to be worth at least a million and a half." Bobby Morton weighed in on the side of his partner.

"I inherited it."

"If not money, what about love, or hate?" Kang changed tack. "You don't have any family, and you said there's no one in your life."

"That's right, there's no one in my life right now." Felicity forestalled Kang's question. "I broke up with my last boyfriend some time ago. It wasn't pleasant, but it was the right thing to do."

"That's new information, Felicity. What's his name?" Sam asked.

"Tony DiPane. He runs a bakery on Post."

"I'll get someone to check him out." Sam made a note in his book. Detective Kang wrote Tony's name on a flipchart sheet.

"I don't think he would have done this. He's a philanderer, not a killer." Felicity didn't like having to defend her ex.

"Maybe not the killer, but don't you think he might be in danger of being a victim?" Kang twisted his lips in scorn. "So, now we have new information on the board, but it doesn't clear you."

Felicity struggled again with her temper. Couldn't they see that they were wasting time? "I wouldn't do this. Look, either you believe I am Wiccan and follow the tenets of my belief, or you don't. If you don't believe it, then you can't expect me to provide insight into his mind. If you do, then you know I can't be sitting here if I had done this." She pointed to the flipchart paper headed Wicca. "The rule of three. If I killed even one of these people I would receive the pain and disfigurement back three times over."

"Right," Kang snorted. "Just because you believe it doesn't mean it will happen."

Esther interrupted, the argument. "Let's not go down this path any further. It's not productive. We agree, I think, on the fact that this is being done by a man. Felicity is obviously a woman. Let's move on."

"Just because some guy did the work doesn't mean she isn't involved." It seemed Kang was not letting go of his theory.

"I don't see why you keep pushing on this idea." Felicity felt her control slip. "I didn't do it. If you have proof, or even reasonable evidence, that I did have something to do with it, then arrest me. Otherwise I'm going. We're not getting anywhere, and I have other things to do with my time."

"Nothing I can use yet," Kang said before anyone could step in and defuse the situation.

"And you won't." Felicity stood up and took her coat and purse from the back of the chair. "I'm going home. I hope you'll get your act together and start looking for this maniac before he reaches thirteen bodies. Something is going to happen at that point, and I can't predict what that might be."

She slammed the door open and stood waiting for Sam.

She heard Sam snap at Kang. "You wonder why we don't

cooperate. I thought you agreed she wasn't a suspect. If we aren't going in the same direction on this investigation, we won't need to share information. I didn't agree with the orders to work together on this investigation. I can talk to my director if you don't want to team up. Esther, come on, we'll drive you back to your office."

TWENTY-FOUR

Sid stood in the shadows across the street from Felicity's window. Thanking the Lord and Lady for the fact that the window looked into the kitchen, he watched her reach into the cupboard and take a can of soup. He licked his lips as he watched her open it and pour the contents into a saucepan. She moved about the kitchen setting the table with a bowl, spoon, and napkin. Watching her graceful movements brought memories of the first time he had seen her.

He was walking back from renting the warehouse, not yet sure why he needed the space. Industrial Street was a long walk from home, but in those days, he had nothing but time and a compulsion to find a quiet location.

The decision to wander through the SoMa district changed his life. She had been balancing a cardboard tray of coffee cups. While he watched in awe, the wind took her auburn curls and tossed them all around her face. He remembered the music of her laughter as she used one hand to pull the hair out of her eyes. The world had seemed to stop spinning. Time to stop running. He remembered the thud of his heart, and the sudden absence of the normal city hum. She was perfect. When the sunlight touched her hair, he saw the aura of the goddess.

He had almost rushed to kneel at her feet. Something stopped him. He knew that her love would have to be earned. If he were ready, she would have seen him, beckoned him over. But she seemed unaware that her most devoted disciple was standing only ten feet away. Sid knew it was a test. The Goddess knew he was here. How could she not? He would have to sacrifice something to gain her attention. Now he understood the urge to rent the warehouse. It would become his church. He took a picture of the doorway she passed through. An older building, in this part of town it would be full of small businesses. He would start his research there. He would know the name she bore on Earth before he slept.

The chill of the night brought Sid back to the present. He still longed to reach out to her, to ask what test she was setting him.

"Soon. Soon I will sit at your feet and adore you." He fingered the phone in his pocket and looked across the shadows to the car where two FBI agents sat. They couldn't see him. He had come to this spot from their blind side. In a half hour or so, one of the two would step out of the car and walk around the block. Sid would be gone by then. Long gone.

Now she was at the table, sipping soup and flipping through the pages of a magazine. Sid was overwhelmed with a desire to hear her speak. He pulled the phone out of his pocket and dialed her number.

The phone rang twice before Felicity moved out of his line of sight.

"Hello." Her voice was warm, and Sid felt a sudden panic. He was not yet good enough to speak to her. He clicked the phone shut.

Felicity returned to the table, but now she wasn't eating. Sid felt the compulsion to talk to her again. "You've upset her," he muttered. "You must calm her down."

He pressed the talk button twice and waited. This time he watched her jump out of the chair and run for the phone.

"Hello?" Her voice was now full of fear. "Hello? Who are you? I can hear you breathe. What do you want?"

Sid snapped the phone shut. What had he done? He prayed that he hadn't destroyed everything he'd worked for, that he would not have to start again. Or, worse, that she would judge him unworthy. He glanced back at the car. The agents were staring at the house. They could see the same thing as he had. Sid took a step backwards, careful to move smoothly and stay out of the agents' line of sight.

FELICITY STOOD TREMBLING, the phone in hand. She had finally been able to relax the fear that she felt strangling her. The presence of the agents outside was enough to stop her jumping at every sound the old house made. She hadn't felt exactly normal, but closer to it than she had come in weeks. She knew the call was from the murderer. It couldn't be a coincidence. "Get hold of yourself," she said, dialing Sam's number.

He answered before the first ring ended. "Felicity, what is it?"

She gulped for breath, her precarious control slipping. "I just got two hang ups. I think it was him. I don't know why, but it feels like he's watching me. The second time the phone rang right when I sat back at the table."

"I'm on my way. Can you see the team in the car?" His words came out hard and fast.

She went to the bay window and looked across the street. "Yes."

"Flick your lights on and off. They'll come to you."

"Done." Felicity kept her focus on the agents crossing the street, trying not to imagine a killer lurking nearby. "They're coming."

"Okay, when they get inside, tell them what happened. I'll be there in five minutes. Don't hang up until the agents are inside."

"Don't worry, I won't." Hearing Sam on the phone slowed her racing heart, she didn't feel alone as long as he was in contact. She tried not to think what life would be like when he was gone back to New York. The only people she could call friends now were her employees, and George. Sam was filling a void she didn't know existed.

AFTER TELLING the two agents what had happened, Felicity gratefully followed the instruction to sit on the couch and stay away from the windows.

When he arrived, Sam held a hushed conversation with agents Smith and Johnson that ended with an order to check the area. Then he sat on the couch next to her and pulled her close, drawing her into his arms. "It's okay. You're safe. I'm here."

Felicity felt the pain of all her tension in her throat and then the heat of tears falling and soaking Sam's shirt. "I'm sorry. I thought I was going to be okay," she sobbed.

"No one is okay with this. The bureau trains us to deal with it, but even we're not okay with it." He eased back to look at her face, wiping her cheeks. "I'll be here tonight. And the team is moving inside tomorrow."

"No, I don't want to be..." She checked her knee jerk reaction of independence. "I mean, yes, thank you. It makes more sense, and I'll be safer. I will live with it. At least it's only until we catch this guy."

"Yes, you'll be safer." Sam shook his head and pulled her closer. "It's the only thing that is important right now."

Felicity slowed her breathing, making sure her tears had ceased before she pulled away from Sam's embrace. "Thanks. I'm sorry I fell apart. I guess the phone calls just brought the situation home to me."

"It will keep coming back as long as this guy is out there. I'm sorry, Felicity, I wish we could figure out who he is." Sam leaned back on the sofa and rubbed his eyes with the heels of his hands. "Are you sure you haven't noticed anyone hanging around?"

"No. I mean, yes, I'm sure. But I keep thinking about it, and now I'm starting to imagine things, I think." She shivered.

"Like what? Sometimes memory feels like imagination."

"Like the coffee guy seems to be chattier than usual. Like the delivery man for the courier seems to wait until Isaac leaves before he delivers a package. Like the taxi driver the other day seemed to take the long way around, and I wonder if it was just to be with me longer." She sighed. "It's all paranoia. None of those things are valid."

"Probably not." Sam looked up at the creak of a step. "I'll get it." He took out his gun. "You head to the bedroom until I say it's clear."

Felicity stood in the doorway of her bedroom.

"Agent Barton, it's Johnson." She heard. Sam put the gun down at his side, but not back in the shoulder holster. "What's the code?"

"Gandalf."

Sam opened the door and both Smith and Johnson entered. "Anything?"

"No. We walked the whole block. There's no evidence that anyone spent a lot of time standing around anywhere. If he hung out for anytime he didn't leave any cigarette butts or candy wrappers."

"There's no pay phone nearby either." Agent Smith added.

"Okay, call it in and get someone to trace incoming calls to this number. I'll stay tonight. You can head home after the trace. We probably need you to move in tomorrow until we find the perp." The two agents nodded and left.

Sam turned to where Felicity was standing. "I thought I told you to wait in the bedroom."

"Gandalf?" She felt her lips quirk into a quick grin.

"We needed a safe code so you know who is at the door." Sam grinned. "Gandalf or the White Witch were the choices we came up with."

"Very funny," she said. "What good is the code if you didn't tell me?"

"I was about to call to let you know, but you called me first." He threw his coat over the back of the couch. "Let's get back to what we were talking about."

"That would be my paranoia." She went to the kitchen, poured the cold soup into the sink, and plugged in the kettle. "Tea? Coffee?"

"I'll try tea." Sam answered as he came to the kitchen behind her. He took the mugs she'd put on a tray and placed them on the table. "What do you have to eat? I missed supper."

"There are some cookies in the cupboard." She opened the fridge. "I can make you an omelet. Have some cookies while you wait. I don't want my protector to faint with hunger at the wrong moment."

Sam munched chocolate chip cookies while she made the omelet. When the eggs were cooked, she handed him the plate and sat beside him while he ate. "Do you expect to get information about him from my phone records?"

"It's a long shot. He probably has a throwaway phone, but you never know." He wolfed the omelet down and reached for another cookie. "He has to make a mistake at some point. They always do."

"Okay." She took a cookie from the bag. "I've been trying to think if maybe I know this guy. But I haven't a clue what to look for. How would I know who it might be?"

"He probably has been active for a month or so." Sam dipped another cookie in his tea. "We know there are more bodies than we've found. We're not sure why he's started dumping them in public places."

"So, someone new in my life since the beginning of August." She sipped her tea, enjoying the feeling of belonging Sam brought to her home. She hadn't realized it was missing until now. "I haven't hired any new temps lately. We need people, so Isaac has been screening applicants, but I haven't met any of them."

"Get me the list of people he's screened. Maybe someone saw you without you knowing."

"I suppose. We've gained two new clients in that time. Neither of them seemed interested in anything more than getting temporary help, though. I'll get Isaac to give you their information."

"It's worth checking them out. I'll be discreet. I don't want to cost you a client unnecessarily."

"I can't think of anyone else new." Felicity yawned, realizing she felt safe enough to relax.

"You should go to bed. I'll be here. You can sleep." He reached out and pushed her hair behind her ear. Felicity smiled. In other circumstances Sam wouldn't be sleeping on the couch. "You might be able to think more clearly in the morning."

"Hmm." She looked out of the window. "I hope so. I should have asked before; did you get in touch with Tony?"

"He's out of town. We went to the bakery and talked to his

assistant." Sam chuckled again. "You have to love that name; Tony DiPane. Tony the Bread and he's a baker."

"I know we used to laugh about the fact he had a built-in mob name." Felicity cleared the table as she spoke.

Sam looked up. "Did he need a mob name?"

"No, he didn't. Other than cheating on me, he lived a very honest life." She yawned again and sat down.

"He was a fool to lose you," Sam said.

"That's a nice thing to say," Felicity murmured, half asleep in the chair.

Sam cleared his throat. "Anyway, his assistant said Tony was scheduled to go on vacation for two weeks, and he left on Monday. We're trying to find out how to contact him." He watched Felicity's eyes close.

"Tony might be at his aunt's in Florence. That's where he usually went on vacation. I have the number in an old address book. It's at the office. We can go there now if you think it will help."

"Tomorrow morning will be fine. Go to bed before you fall asleep here." Sam nodded his chin toward the bedroom. "I'll turn on the TV to keep awake. I'll have the sound low, so don't worry if you hear voices."

"You're right I'm about to start snoring."

Sam helped her out of the chair and led her to the bedroom. On the way, she found the remote control and showed him where she kept the coffee beans in case he needed a jolt of caffeine in the night.

SID HELD HIMSELF STILL. The agents missed him when they checked the street, looking right past him as though he were a ghost. He knew where to hide, and he knew how to get back to this one spot where he could see her. Should he call again? No. The thought of calling her, twisted his stomach with nervous energy. He could wait until Mabon.

Movement in her kitchen caught his attention. A man was making coffee. It was that FBI agent, Sam Barton. Sid had learned all he could about Sam as soon as he heard his name. Sam could be a problem. Now he was in the Goddess's house, and that was wrong. This was something Sid could not accept, but he'd found the Mabon sacrifice he needed to complete the spell. With that sacrifice, he could bind the Goddess Felicity to him for life. He would not stand across the street after that. He would be in the kitchen. He would be preparing food and drink for his Goddess.

Now he needed to complete tonight's sacrifice. Sid turned and left through the shadows the way he had come.

TWENTY-FIVE

"Are you feeling better?" Sam asked as he passed Felicity a mug of coffee the next morning.

"Less tired at least." Sleeping through the night hadn't reduced her fears. "Is there any news?"

"The phone calls came from a toss-away phone. So, no help there."

"I didn't get any epiphanies." She heard the disappointment in her voice and tried to feel some optimism.

Sam gave that warm chuckle she felt all the way through her body. "It's a bit too early for epiphanies. Have some breakfast, and then we'll go into your office and get the job applications."

"I'm not hungry."

Sam waved a toasted bagel under her nose. "Just take a couple of bites, and then we'll go."

"Yes, mother." She obediently shoved a piece of the buttered and honeyed bagel into her mouth. Chewing, she grabbed her purse and jacket and waited at the door for Sam.

. . .

THE OFFICE WAS BUZZING with people when they arrived, temps were dropping off signed work receipts, and Isaac was talking to a tall man with faded red hair. The phone rang and Isaac held up a finger to the redhead and answered it.

"Help on Demand, whatever you need, we can get it done." He winked at Sam as they paused beside his desk and made a note on a message pad before hanging up.

"Can you come in when you're done, please?" Felicity asked quietly as she walked through the reception area.

Isaac turned to the man waiting patiently in front of him. "Please have a seat. Fill out this application, and we'll see if we can squeeze in an interview this morning." Then he turned and beamed at Sam. "What can I do for you, Handsome Sam?"

"I'm here too, Isaac." Felicity waved her hand in front of her assistant's face. "Please, remember I'm the one who signs your paycheck."

"Oh, sweetie, don't make me choose between love and money," he said, following them into Felicity's office.

Sam laughed. "No love here, Isaac. Sorry, Felicity's more my type."

Felicity warmed at his words. "Isaac, leave Agent Barton alone."

"Okay, I guess, but I had to try." He turned to Felicity. "Money it is. Not that I don't love you, boss, just not that kind of love. What do you need?"

"We need to see all the applicants for the open slots, and I need Tony's aunt's number. Do you know where my old address book was put?"

"I know exactly which box it's in, I'll get it for you. I'll bring the applications, and there's one more, I'll copy it as soon as he's done." Isaac pointed at the man sitting in the reception area.

Sam pulled a chair up to Felicity's desk when Isaac left.

"While we're waiting tell me about Tony. What else does he do? If he's not at his aunt's house where else might he be?"

"He loves golf and baking. In the day, if he's not at his bakery, he's at the driving range, or on a golf course."

"What about night?"

"Usually in a bar, or at a game if any of the teams are playing at home. I met him at O'Dunnigans, his favorite at the time, but I don't know if it still is. He didn't usually stay out late because he was at the ovens very early every day." Felicity tried to think of anything else that might help Sam.

"What about girlfriends?"

"That I wouldn't know," she admitted. "I caught him cheating with a tourist. I broke it off, walked out, and didn't keep in touch. I was pretty mad for a while and by the time I cooled down it wasn't worth calling him."

"Do you think Tony could be the killer?" Sam kept his gaze on her face.

Ignoring his scrutiny, Felicity snorted. "Oh, no. Tony hated violence and he used to get queasy at the sight of blood. He wouldn't even let me order my steak rare because it made him feel faint."

"People change."

She shrugged. "If he's changed that fundamentally, then I don't know how to help you. All I can say is the Tony I knew wouldn't be able to commit these murders."

Isaac pushed the office door open. "Here's your address book and the seven applications that passed the screen." He put them on the table. "Here are the rest of the ones we received, including today's guy there are twenty. Is there anything else?"

"You know that these people being murdered are connected to Felicity," Sam asked.

"Yes. How awful that must be for you." He looked sympathetically at Felicity. "I'm trying not to be nosy but if you need to talk, honey, I'm here."

"Any idea who might be doing this?" Sam asked.

"Like someone she fought with? God no, Felicity doesn't fight." Isaac threw his arms up in mock horror.

"What about someone who might have been asking questions about her. Anyone seem interested in her. Someone who shouldn't have been?"

Isaac pointed to the two piles of applications. "Most of them asked at least once what she was like to work for. That's kind of natural when you are looking for a job. The guy in the lobby asked a couple of personal questions that seemed odd and he was really interested in that part time position here. But..."

Sam lunged for the door and headed to the lobby. "He's gone."

"Good. He was kind of creepy. I wasn't going to pass him onto you for interviewing." Isaac's eyes widened. "Oh my God, you don't think he might be... Oh my God."

"Maybe not." As Sam looked at Felicity, she felt the blood drain from her face. "Some guys are just creepy."

"That would be a very large coincidence," Felicity muttered, feeling the same way she had the night before with the phone call. That it really was too much of a coincidence.

"Yes." Sam looked at Isaac. "Is that the original application or a copy?"

"Original, I can give you the pen he used if it's still there, and the clipboard if you want it."

"Yes, and don't touch anything else. We'll get fingerprints taken just in case."

"I guess we should count our blessings that it will only be in the reception area. It will be a quick and easy clean up." Isaac went back to his desk, and Sam called the crime scene team.

Felicity motioned Sam to sit back in the chair he'd left.

"While we're waiting, should we assume it was just a coincidence and go through these applicants?"

"First let's try to track down Tony." Sam pointed to the address book. "Why did you put that in the box at the office? Most people keep personal stuff and business stuff separate."

"It contained all my contacts, business and personal." Felicity held up her PDA. "When we got these, Isaac loaded everything in electronically, and we kept the originals, just in case."

"So, why did we need the book?"

"Oh, it was in my angry phase. I told Isaac not to put any of the contacts related to Tony in my PDA." She grinned. "It seems a bit petty now, but it felt like closure when I did it."

She flipped through the book and dialed the number in Italy putting the phone on speaker when it started to ring. "It's seven pm there right now. I should catch them at home. Oh, hello, Gina, it's Felicity. Do you remember me?"

"Yes, *bella*. Tony was stupid to let you get away. How are you, *bene*?"

"*Si, bene, e lei?*"

"I'm wonderful. What can I do for you? Are you coming to *Firenze*?"

"No, Gina, I'm trying to find out where Tony is. Do you know?"

"No, he was supposed to be coming here, but he sent me an email to say his plans changed. Ah, have you forgiven him? You are back together, yes?"

"No, sorry, Gina, I just needed to help someone find him. Will you call me if he contacts you?"

"Of course." The background sounds of people drinking and laughing rose. "*Cara*, I have to go back to my guests. Call me again, I would love to gossip with you. And, think about coming to visit. Just because you are not dating that terrible nephew of mine doesn't mean you aren't welcome here."

"Thank you, I will, *ciao*." Tears of anticipated sadness prickled the back of her eyes, she hoped the next call to Gina would be to make travel plans, not deliver bad news. She blinked the tears away and looked to Sam for the next move.

"I think we keep looking for the killer here." He reached for the pile of rejected candidates. "Isaac wrote the reason they were rejected on the sheet. Do you think he told them why they didn't get an interview?"

"That would depend on why they were rejected."

Sam flipped through the papers and sorted them into piles. "Criminal record, bad reference, lack of skills, not able to contact. People get rejected out of hand for these reasons?"

"Not completely. I remember how hard it is to apply for jobs and not hear back. We do try to touch base even if we aren't interested."

She tapped the first pile. "Criminal record. He would probably have let them know it came up. It could be an error, and they might want to fix it. Bad reference, that depends. If it seems like a personality conflict he might refer them back to the person they gave as a reference. If it was about work habits, he might have asked some questions. Lack of skills, he probably told them then and there. Not able to contact, well that's self-evident."

"Okay, I'll ask him about the reference, and I'll get the information on the criminal records."

They turned their attention to the seven applicants who passed the first screen. "I'll get these down to the office and have the checks redone. Have you set up any interviews?"

"Not yet," she said. "Should we?"

"No. Let's see what the checks turn up before you do

anything more." The sound of voices rose from the reception area. "That sounds like the crime scene team. I'll get some evidence bags for the papers."

TWENTY-SIX

"Too close, too much risk, she might have known you, fool," Sid berated himself. He thought going to her office was a brilliant idea. He had hoped to learn something. Then she walked in. That Sam Barton was with her. Sid felt suspicion emanate from Sam like a stink.

"Stop talking to yourself." He hit the side of his head with a clenched fist. It was important to focus now. It was critical to be careful. This was the last ritual, the one for Mabon. The one that would release the magic he needed, the ritual that would bind him to the Goddess forever.

"For this spell, I will need her essence too. I'll get that tomorrow. I'll need ground bone for the earth. That's what the fingers are for. It will be dried enough for grinding tomorrow."

"Air. Now that will bear thinking about. Maybe perfume, maybe incense, maybe something else. Fire. Oil lantern, I think the glass one would be best. Water, something potent, ah, yes," Sid picked up a bottle wrapped in burlap. "Consecrated wine, perfect." He knew when he stole it from the church it would be important.

He reached up into the cupboard for paper, pen, and ink to write the note. Then he put them aside. Next, he reached for, and opened, the hardbound book. "Mabon rituals." He read what his grandfather had written in his childish block letters. "Harvest, time to reap rewards of hard work and sacrifice for the honor of the Lord and Lady. Bigger the sacrifice, bigger the honor, bigger the reward for the faithful."

Sid smiled. A special agent of the FBI was as big a sacrifice as he'd ever attempted. He lit a candle and the scent of cinnamon filled the room. Pulling a whetstone from the cupboard, Sid began sharpening the knife. The last sacrifice had been intricate and the edge was dull. As he sharpened he muttered, "God and Goddess, Lord and Lady, Father and Mother of all life, I present this anthame for your approval and ask that it be used in your service." He stopped sharpening the tool and closed his eyes breathing deeply for a minute.

Reaching for the bottle, he poured a few drops of wine on the blade. Then he passed it through the candle flame.

"May the essence of earth, air, fire, and water cleanse and purify this anthame so that it may be used in your service. So mote it be." He took the now sharpened knife and laid it across his open palms. He raised them to shoulder height and bowed his head. "I charge this anthame by the thousands of names of our Lord and Lady and ask that They accept it in Their service. So mote it be."

As he lay the knife on the black velvet cloth, it slid and cut the fleshy part of his left thumb. "No, no, no." Sid sucked the blood from his palm. Using his right hand, he turned the knife over, looking for traces of his blood. The smear of red on the blade brought tears of frustration.

He wrapped his hand until the bleeding stopped. He filled a bowl with bleach and submerged the anthame. "Stupid. Careless." He slapped himself again.

After leaving it in the bleach for a half hour, he wiped the knife clean and started the consecration ritual again. When he finished, Sid wrapped the knife in the black velvet cloth, then snuffed the flame of the candle between his fingers. He replaced the cork before putting the bottle on the shelf. Then he checked the contents of the drawers.

"Oil for the flames. Sage, pine, and sandalwood incense, all powerful choices, any of those will do for air. The bones will need a filler there's not quite enough to make the circle whole. I should have sacrificed him sooner. More time to dry more bones." Taking the baker's bones for the next sacrifice had been inspired. Proof that the goddess was with him. It felt like he'd risen above his limitations and that his grandfather would be proud. "Something as powerful as bone, but one that will not conflict. Salt might do. But something more volatile would be better. I have some time to think about it. No rush. No rush."

"How do I take him? He's big, and he carries a gun. I will need to be careful." Sid opened the last drawer and looked over the vials of prescription medicine he had taken from clients over the years when he'd been a home care worker. There were packages of powder he'd bought on the streets that he used to keep his sacrifices from losing consciousness too soon.

This time he needed something to temporarily incapacitate his victim, not keep him awake. He took one vial out. "Rohypnol. Maybe, but I have time to think of something better. I can't chance that he'll stay awake. He must be unconscious and harmless until I need him."

Sid placed all his equipment on the solid table in the corner of the room. The table was draped in red cloth. There were darker stains on the top of the cloth. Testaments to the blood he'd shed in the name of the Goddess.

He needed to check on the finger bones that he'd left in the office. He wiped his hands on the seat of his jeans and went upstairs. The dehydrator was still running. "Good, good." He looked through the clear glass and saw that the bones looked properly leached out. Four days of dehydration, the bones were probably ready for grinding. Sid turned the machine off.

He patted the top. "Tomorrow we'll grind. I think." He pulled a notebook and pencil out of the drawer. "What crime should I drive from his body first? He may have despoiled her, but maybe not. I must choose the right sin."

Sid sat scribbling words on paper and then discarding them for an hour before he decided on the right words. "He has blocked my access to her. All these other sins are part of that greater offence. If he was not there, I would have comforted her and she would have loved me before the final rite. We could have performed the Mabon ritual together."

He scribbled 'agent of the devil' in the notebook. "He needs to be cleansed of his master. When I've accomplished that, she will belong to me. She will see me as a savior."

Sid wrote his ritual out to allow him to memorize it in time for Mabon. *I call thee Lady to this circle...*

When he'd finished drafting the ritual, he turned to another page and wrote a new note. This note would be different. This note he would hand to Felicity after the ritual. This note didn't only record the ritual. It formed part of the ritual.

THE DEVIL ENTERED *this body an age ago. He took it on himself to stand between you and your servants. He barred you from your true role in this world and endangered your eternal soul.*

Lord and Lady turn your backs. He confined your aspect on Earth

. . .

WHEN HE BELIEVED the wording was perfect, Sid ripped out the page and took it with him downstairs. He then carefully copied the note onto a vellum sheet, using his own blood for ink.

TWENTY-SEVEN

"Hey, I see you've already cleaned up," Sam said as he entered Felicity's office.

Felicity laughed. "Yes, well, your cleaning team did most of it, but we're getting good at this."

"It's good to hear you laugh," Sam said. "It will help you get through this."

"If I thought crying would help, I'd be weeping an ocean. The victims have gone to their own versions of the Summerlands. I can't change that." She knew that she was only holding her tears at bay temporarily. There were many days of mourning ahead of her. "Do you have any more information?"

"They found four sets of fingerprints that weren't yours or Isaac's." Sam pulled the door shut. "We haven't identified anyone yet."

"I've been thinking about that. It seems like every time we think there's a lead it ends up as nothing. What about getting more aggressive?" She held her breath waiting for Sam's reaction.

He looked at her, eyes narrowed. "What do you mean?" She could hear suspicion in his voice.

Felicity lowered her eyes to focus on the desk. Her nerve wouldn't survive seeing Sam's anger. "What if we tried to entice him out rather than wait from him to make a mistake?"

"No."

"Wait Sam, hear me out." Glancing up, Felicity saw his mouth press shut.

Sam's voice was hard when he answered, "No. It's too dangerous."

"For whom?" she snapped, putting aside her worry that he would react badly since they were in the middle of it.

"For you." Sam crossed his arms across his chest. "At least, if I'm guessing right, and you would be part of the plan to entice him out."

"Well he does seem to be fixated on me. I am the perfect choice." She kept her voice even, not wanting to tip it into an argument, but ready to keep the subject going until he backed down. No matter what she was feeling for Sam, or he was feeling for her, it was not going to prevent her from trying to stop this maniac.

Sam leaned forward across her desk. "No. I can't authorize it. It's too dangerous. We don't even like to send agents in as bait. Why would we let you do that?"

"At some point, it won't be up to you, Sam. He's going to escalate it to include me anyway by this time next week." Felicity was counting on the fact that her ability to be stubborn would outlast Sam's objections. It all made sense to her, keeping her safe was not worth someone's life. Sam would understand eventually.

"Maybe, maybe not, it's all theory. He might just move on somewhere else. This could all be about setting up for some magic event that won't happen." Sam's chin jutted and his eyes seemed to burn through Felicity.

"You know that's unlikely. He does all the work, and all the research he needs to make sure that everything works for him. He's not going to be leaving his goal up to chance. He's got something planned. I don't want to leave it up to him anymore." She refused to react to the way he was ignoring her idea.

"What part of *no* don't you understand? It's not going to change." He stepped around her desk. "You can't do this."

"It's not like I will do this on my own," she continued, struggling to keep forcing the emotions out of her tone. "You'll be there, or another agent. I will be protected."

"Perhaps we're not speaking the same language. No, non, nyet, nein, nuh uh." He crossed his arms firmly over his chest. "I don't want you close to this guy. It's not safe."

"Don't be so stubborn." She shook her head. "Look, you can't stop me. I can find a way to get him to come to me if I have to. I thought you'd want to make sure I was safe. But if not, then don't get in my way."

She watched the emotions cross Sam's face. When she saw his hesitation, she knew she'd won. "Damn you." Sam's voice rose. "I'll have you arrested as a suspect. This is way too dangerous. I don't want to lose you."

"You won't." Felicity reached out and touched his crossed arms. "Sam, I don't want to lose you either, and I don't want to become another victim. I do want to survive this. I just can't sit by and wait any longer. It's driving me crazy. I am not the kind of person who just sits back."

He seemed to drop his resistance. "I'm not making any promises. I don't like any idea that will put you in jeopardy. I'll listen. Tell me your plan." He leaned his arms on the desktop.

"I think he's been killing people close to me so I will be alone. He wants me to be vulnerable or leave me with no options. What if we put someone new in his way?" She waited, trying not to push too hard for Sam to agree.

Sam uncrossed his arms. "Okay, that makes some sense."

"So, if he thought you and I were getting to be a couple..." She could feel her face warm at the thought.

"Then he'd come after me," Sam finished. "Not a bad plan. It keeps you out of the action."

"Yes." Felicity didn't add that she planned to be very much in the center of the action. "I'm not happy that you will be in the middle of it."

"At least I have a gun. And training."

"Sam, don't get too comfortable with that. A gun is no guarantee. It's just an advantage."

He smiled and heat rose in Felicity's chest. "I know. I promise I won't get complacent."

"Good. If he thinks we are getting close, I hope it will push him over the edge. And if he's looking to finalize the plan on Mabon, he might have to act quickly to get you prepared."

"As much as I hate the idea of putting you closer to him, I have to agree, the plan is solid. But it's not up to me. I'll need to get approval. Would you be okay if we put a lookalike in your place?"

"Do you really think he'll be fooled?" Felicity knew what the answer should be. She hoped Sam did too.

"Not really." Sam shook his head. "Look I still think it's crazy, but since the plan doesn't put you in the hot seat I'll propose it."

"Thanks." Felicity tried to ignore the shiver of fear that crossed her shoulders. "When will you know? Time is going pretty quickly."

"I'll talk to my boss as soon as I can. He'll need to talk to his boss." Sam ran his hands through his hair making a mess of waves. "I'll come by the house tomorrow with the answer."

TWENTY-EIGHT

The fog was rolling back into the water when the garbage trucks rumbled into the street. Fisherman's wharf and Pier 39 were big tourist attractions, and that meant lots of garbage. Candy wrappers, take-out boxes, souvenir shop bags, and pop cans overflowed the municipal containers. The city wanted the street cleaned early in the morning, so tourists didn't wade through piles of trash on their way to the restaurants, shops, and ferry terminals.

Melissa didn't particularly like the early morning run on the trucks, but it meant she got the rest of the day free to work on her thesis. Without a job to get up for in the morning she knew she would end up sleeping until noon and wasting most of her productive time warming up for the day.

The garbage truck slowed to a stop outside Tarantino's restaurant. "I'll take the water side of the street," she shouted to the man on the other side of the truck before she jumped off the back and ran to the nearest bin.

The smell didn't bother her anymore. She'd become used to it after her first week. There were the usual crowd of seagulls flocking around the garbage, and she waved her arms to disperse them before unlatching the lid.

The bag felt heavier than usual, and when she lifted it, something shifted to the bottom of the bag. It felt like someone had dumped a tree branch in the bin. She took the last few steps away from the bin, swung the bag into the back of the truck, and saw the contents spill out.

"Stop," she screamed as she banged on the back of the truck and ran around the side. "Damn, stop. There was an arm in that bag. Don't mash."

The truck stopped moving, and the driver climbed out to look. They weren't supposed to climb up the side of the truck to look in, but when the truck stopped, it was safe enough.

"Crap, yep, it's at least part of an arm," the driver confirmed. "Hang on, and I'll call the cops. It might be another one of those satanic murders that was in the paper." He spat on the pavement as he walked back to the cab to make the call.

Sam received the call as he was picking up coffee to take to Felicity. "Damn. I'll be there in ten minutes. Keep the scene clear, and don't let anyone leave until I get there."

He put the coffee tray on the passenger seat and drove down to Jefferson Street. The early traffic was backing up because of the closure of the road. This was going to be a long day of holding back the tourists and the press.

"What have we got," he asked Bobby Morton. The cop was standing beside a pretty blonde in a city uniform.

Bobby moved away from her before answering, "It's the worst so far. He chopped the body up into pieces. I think the fingers are gone. We haven't found one yet." Bobby was pale. A sheen of sweat covered his face. "I think we're gonna be finding body parts all over the place."

"Did anyone see anything?" Sam asked, looking around the scene.

"No. Just like before, no blood, body mutilated, way more than before, and dumped when no one was around."

"He's not helping us at all, is he?" Sam looked around again. There were plenty of ways to get onto the street without anyone noticing you were carrying a body. "Can we get a team looking around the side streets just in case?"

"Yeah. Maybe he made a mistake. It's bound to happen sometime. I think we'd all be happier if it happened sooner rather than later." Bobby motioned to three uniformed cops standing next to the garbage truck. "Check out the streets as far as you can, do the alleyways too. Look for the missing body parts and see if you can find anything else that might relate to the body. Don't forget that might include the clothes." The uniformed men spread out.

Bobby turned to Sam. "How's your young lady?"

"She's not my young lady," Sam responded, despite the warmth that filled him at the words. "I don't mix dating with protection. She's getting more feisty. She's coming up with plans to catch him."

"Shit, that's usually not good."

"Well, it's not a bad plan, but it means she's putting herself on the line. The problem is my supervisor approved it." Sam shook his head. "Do we know who this victim is?"

"No. No fingers. No prints."

"My guess is this is her ex-boyfriend. He's been missing. She thinks there's one more to come by Friday; or on Friday."

"You going to ask her to identify the body?"

"Not if I can help it. Was there anything about it I can use if I ask her for distinguishing marks?"

"There's a tattoo that has been there for a while. It's pretty cut up but it looks like it was a picture of a poppy. There was some writing with it but the carving made such a mess of it that no one can make out what it said."

"Who found the body?"

"Garbage woman." He pointed at the blonde. "Melissa Acroyd. She noticed it as it fell out of the bag into the truck."

"Was the whole body in the same bag?"

"No, we found a leg already in the truck. Her partner had thrown the first bag in. The torso was leaning against another container, and the other limbs were across the street in one bin."

"The head?"

"Yeah. That was sitting on the sidewalk. Dogs or something had gotten to it in the night. It's pretty chewed up."

Sam looked over the railing. The boats bobbed up and down with the waves as if nothing was different. Three harp seals were watching the activity on the street. "Get someone on the dock."

"I did already."

"Okay." Sam shuddered. This was hitting new highs in gruesome. "I'll talk to Ms. Acroyd, and then I'll go over to Felicity's."

Sam asked Melissa Acroyd the usual questions. Certain that he'd get the same answers Bobby did, but needing to get his own reading on what she had to say. He looked at the body pieces laid out on plastic sheets and made a few notes about the different markings. On the way to Felicity's house, far enough away that it wouldn't contaminate the scene any more than it already was, he threw the coffee in a garbage container. The smell had started to turn his stomach.

TWENTY-NINE

Sam arrived at her front door and before he could knock, she opened it. "What are you doing?" he snapped. "You don't open the door without getting ID or the password. Where are the agents I left here?" He pushed his way through the door.

"Here, Sam. Don't worry we saw you pull up," agent Smith called from the living room.

"Not good enough. There's a maniac out there and he's going to come for her sooner or later." Sam tried to get control of his temper. These were experienced agents. She really wasn't in danger. He was letting his attraction to her get in the way. But all that reasoning didn't calm his fear that Felicity would end up as one more body scattered somewhere in the city.

"Okay, calm down." Smith got up and stood by the front door. "I'll watch the street." He lowered his voice as he passed Sam, his eyebrow raised to accompany his question. "I guess something happened?"

"Yes. Let me break it to her." Sam took a deep breath and let go of the final dregs of anger. It wouldn't help when he talked to Felicity.

"What is it?" Felicity stood in the doorway to the kitchen. "Just tell me. Don't think about how to break it to me."

"There's been another body."

"Where? I want to see it." She picked up her purse and started for the door.

"No. Believe me you don't." Sam took her arm and led her to the couch. "We haven't identified him yet. But is there anything that might tell us if is or isn't Tony?"

"He has a tattoo." Felicity felt a certainty fall on her heart. "It was a poppy with the words 'not just a flower underneath.'"

"I'm sorry," Sam said.

"Lord and Lady protect him on his way to the Summerlands." Felicity closed her eyes as she spoke.

Sam could see tears start to flow down her cheeks.

"I have more news," Sam continued when she opened her eyes, seeing pain there, he added, "It's better news."

"What is it?" Felicity kept her voice level, but he could hear the strain in it.

"I spoke to my supervisor. He okayed the plan you came up with."

She wiped her face and squared her shoulders. "Smart man. When do we start?"

"Are you okay?" He knew the real answer would be no.

"I feel like crap," she admitted. "I am just sitting here with you protecting me, with your gun, and badge. Another one of my friends could be in danger of a truly horrible death, and I'm hiding."

"You're not hiding." Sam waited for the tears to start again.

"Stop looking at me like I'm going to fall apart." Felicity jumped up and started pacing the room. "I don't think I'm going to break down. I'm dry. No more tears. I need to do something, not just sit here." She bumped into the coffee table and spilled the stack of magazines onto the floor. "Ow, Damn!"

Sam reached down to pick up the magazines, and a sheet of vellum slid out onto the floor. "Stop moving."

Felicity stopped rubbing her shin and stared at the paper. "Is that what I think it is?" Her voice was a whisper.

"It looks like it. When did you look at this magazine last?"

"It's new today, it came in the mail."

Sam tried to keep calm, to keep Felicity calm, but his heart stopped beating for a second. "Okay, maybe he wasn't in the house. Maybe he got at the mail before it was delivered. He could work for the distribution house."

"Yes, maybe." Her voice shook. "What does it say?"

Sam used the magazine to lift and slide the note onto the coffee table top.

"Sam, what does it say?" Her voice caught.

"Wait." Sam shook the magazine to make sure there were no other notes. Only two subscription forms fell out. He reached for the two other magazines that hit the floor. A second note was sitting between them. "When did these other ones come?"

"That one yesterday and that last week." The color drained from her face. Sam reached up to catch her, thinking she was going to faint. "He was here. When was he here?" Her voice was a whisper.

"When did you stack the magazines?" Sam rubbed her icy hands to bring back the circulation.

"Yesterday before I went to work. I guess that's good. At least he wasn't creeping around when I was asleep."

"I guess it means he wasn't ready to do anything to you either." Sam paused. "You can't stay here alone any more. Now will you move out?"

"No!" She pulled her hands away. "Sam, I know you want me safe, and it's not that I don't see the sense. But if we're going to go through with the plan, we can't move me. He's watching this house. I think we can be sure of that."

"Then someone is in here all the time. Not just when you are here."

"Won't it scare him off?"

"He's probably expecting it. If we don't react to this, he'll get suspicious." Sam knew he didn't care if they spooked the creep. He needed Felicity to be safe.

"Okay." She touched his arm and smiled. "Maybe you should move in. That would send him a message."

"Do you think he would buy that you'd let me move in just like that? I don't think we can count on him jumping to the conclusion we're dating."

"You're right. We need to let him see us date. We don't have a lot of time, but it's enough to build up some credibility for the cover story." She looked at the notes, biting her lips. "Let's keep going. Read them, maybe there's something that will help."

Sam leaned over and read each one aloud. *"You asked for meat and he gave you fish. Now he serves at Satan's table. Lord and Lady turn your backs. He disobeyed your aspect on Earth."*

Sam looked at Felicity. "Any idea who this might be?"

"No," she said before frowning. "Well maybe. I got takeout a few weeks back and when I got home, it was the wrong order. It happens occasionally. I can't believe he knew about it."

"He's been doing a lot of research." Sam gritted his teeth, forcing himself to move on to read the next note. *"He claimed he loved you but he lied. Your heart was broken and now he lies to the lord of flies. Lord and Lady turn your backs. He wounded your aspect on Earth."*

Felicity shuddered. "Tony."

Sam pointed to the last note. *"She sat too close to you in your heart. She was no acolyte she worshipped a different Lord. Now she sits at the feet of her false god. Lord and Lady turn your backs. She failed your aspect on Earth."*

"It must be Amelie. I don't know what he might be referring to but the 'close to you in your heart' could be about friendship."

"Yes, I guess that gives us four missing bodies. There are twelve people dead and if you are right, there's one more to come next week." He walked to the door in answer to the bell. "Dorothy."

"Emerald City," the answer came back. Sam opened the door to the forensic team. He pointed them to the coffee table and the notes and drew Felicity into the kitchen. "Can you check for bugs, too? If he's been listening in on us, we're screwed."

"Dorothy? What happened to Gandalf?" she asked.

"It changes every day. We don't give it to you because you aren't opening the door to anyone."

"What? I'm not supposed to do anything without permission?"

"That's right. Until this guy is caught, you will let us take care of visitors," Sam said.

"But—"

"No but. Let's talk about this plan of yours."

"Yes, the one you got permission to put into action." Felicity seemed far too eager to get on a dangerous road for Sam's comfort. "What if there is a bug?"

"Then he's heard about it and we will have to think of something else. If there's no bug, we need to plan. I don't like it, but we do have permission." Sam resigned himself to putting her in danger.

Felicity looked surprised. "Aren't you going to tell me it's too dangerous? That I'm not safe here. I'm not safe anywhere I bet. This man was able to get into my home. He'll come to get me if I don't go out to get him."

Sam held up his hands in surrender. "Slow down. Let me make my own argument. You're on the wrong track."

"Okay." She sat back and waited for Sam to speak.

"I didn't agree with the decision to go ahead right away, true. But you're right, the fact he's been in your house changes things. I think we need to draw him out, push his buttons. Try to make him slip up before he takes his next victim. If not, it should make him pick me for the final ritual."

"So, when do we start?"

"If we work on the assumption that he's watching you, we need to make it more public than dating would normally be." He looked out the window. "We'll need to act fast and get the surveillance team back in the car. What I said about having people in the house all the time won't work. He's probably picking out the next victim already."

"No bugs," one of the techs confirmed after walking through every room with a sensor.

Sam nodded his thanks then turned back to Felicity. "Your old boyfriend was the last victim. Why wouldn't he want your new boyfriend?" He grinned at her. He could see tenuous grip she held on her emotions in the tremble in her hands as she pulled her hair into a knot.

Felicity swallowed and seemed to push away the sadness. "I guess it makes sense. Do you think he'd wonder that I was dating so soon after Tony's body is found?"

"I don't think he sees that kind of stuff. He only sees what he wants to see and doesn't need any evidence to support his version of the truth." Sam hoped he was right, much better to have the maniac come after him than Felicity.

"How do we get started?"

"Agent Smith is on his way over. When he gets here I'll take off and come back this afternoon and he'll know by then that we're a couple."

"Do you think he's watching now?"

"Maybe, I don't see anyone but he's good at hiding. Why?"

"No reason," Felicity said.

The doorbell rang and Sam heard the passwords exchanged between one of the crime scene techs and agent Smith. Grabbing his jacket, Sam said goodbye to agent Smith as he headed out the door.

"Sam, wait," Felicity called as she ran out to the porch. "Don't be long." She grabbed his shoulders and planted a kiss on him that woke emotions he was trying to keep locked away.

THIRTY

Sam still felt the kiss lingering when he met with Esther that afternoon. They were sitting in the conference room, the walls still covered with sheets of information and pictures of the bodies. He felt the familiar worry that, at some point, the sight of these bodies wouldn't register with him anymore. Maybe it was time to leave the FBI and find a less dehumanizing job.

"Yes, I think it's probable that he's watching her," Esther said her voice cutting through his thoughts.

"Do you think we can count on him watching enough to fall for this?" Sam asked.

"Like I said before, there're no guarantees." She tapped her pen on the side of the table. "We're working under a set of assumptions. First, she's right about the number of victims, and there'll be one more on the twenty second. And he hasn't yet picked the victim. And he's starting to get closer to her."

"Yep, except I think he's been stalking her for a few months. Based on the information he has, it looks like he's been researching her. Not all of what he knows could have come from his victims. And now he's escalating. He's getting in her space and doing more damage to the bodies every time he kills. Like he's willing to do whatever it takes to get her attention."

"If we're right, or even just right on the stalking, he will definitely pick you as the next victim as long as you get between him and her." Esther put the pen in her mouth.

Sam nodded, as he tried to put all the information together, worrying that they'd missed something. They had been going over the same ground all afternoon, nothing new, no new connections. "Yep, but we'll grab him before he takes me down."

"You know these things don't go to plan, Sam."

"I know. Look, just tell me what you think is the fastest way to piss this guy off. If we have to wait until next Friday, I think Felicity will go off the edge. She's wound up enough right now." He remembered the way her hands trembled this morning. "I'm not happy that we are letting her step into the line of fire here."

"No. That's pretty clear." Esther smiled. "Just remember you are acting a part, Sam. It's not fair to her to get involved then go back to New York. She's going to be in a mess when it's over. She'll need support, and this guy has taken all her friends. If you just go away, it might break her."

"I may not go back to New York. You know the situation there hasn't changed." Sam looked at Esther who raised her eyebrow. "Don't look at me like that. I'm not apologizing to the bastard who sued me. And I'm not going to get involved with her. I don't need that kind of complication." Sam wondered if it wasn't already too late to make that promise.

"If you say so," Esther said. "As for speeding it up, if he's on a set timeline you may not be able to do that. But start off slowly, like you are hesitating about getting involved with a victim. If he doesn't respond, then push a bit harder. If no reaction after that, then maybe he isn't watching."

"I don't want to think about that. If we haven't figured this out by then we'll have another body pretty soon and no idea how to stop the killer."

Sam called Felicity as he left the station. "I'll be there around seven and then we can make a bit of a deal of leaving for dinner. I think we would have better luck walking to a restaurant. He might get caught following us."

"There's a great bistro four blocks away. I'll make a reservation for tonight. I'll wear something sexy."

Sam ended the conversation hoping the plan would work and this would end tonight.

FELICITY DECIDED on a green silk shirt over a putty colored tee shirt all paired with charcoal cotton Capri pants. Not exactly sexy, but she'd never been the type to flaunt it. Shoes were the most important choice. She wanted to be comfortable for the walk, but it was supposed to be a first date. If the killer was watching, it would be important that she make the right choice.

She put on the left foot of a pair of slide-on sandals in black leather and the right foot of a grey patent leather Mary Janes. Both were flat heels and would be appropriate, neither were going to make her look like she was on a date. She reached into the closet and pulled out a pair of high heel grey sling backs. Now she was edging into sexy.

She was glad when Sam arrived at five to seven, the waiting was stretching her nerves further than she thought she could stand.

"The team is on the corner in front of the house with green trim. They'll follow us at a discreet distance. If we pick up a tail, they'll see him." Sam handed her a bouquet of mixed flowers in an etched glass vase.

"Thank you, these are lovely. You should come in for a few

minutes." She took his arm and drew him into the room. "If we just run off as soon as you arrive it might not look natural. We have to assume he's looking in on us."

She placed the vase on the coffee table. "Sit down, and have a glass of wine. White or red?"

"Felicity, calm down." Sam patted the couch. "If you run around like that when we're out, you'll tip him off."

"Sorry. I just feel like we are finally getting somewhere." She paused, trying to slow her breathing. "I promise I'll be fine outside. Would you like some wine?"

"Sure, red would be fine." Sam relaxed on the couch, his arms stretched across the back. Felicity poured two glasses of wine and handed Sam his as she sat down.

"How will you know if the team has spotted anything?" she asked.

"We won't know until we get back. The idea is to identify him and find out where he goes. The arrest will come when we know there's no other victim held captive somewhere."

"Okay, so what happens if we spot someone?" She leaned toward Sam, as though flirting.

"*We* do nothing. I have a signal for the team and they will take over." Sam sipped his wine and then placed the glass on the table. "I don't want you trying to do anything. I don't have my gun on me, this is supposed to be a date, remember."

"No gun at all?"

"Okay, yes I have a gun, but it's not obvious, and we're not planning for me to use it."

"Okay, so we're on a date, should we go?" She stood and picked up her purse from the side table.

FELICITY FELT her skin come alive in the breeze. It carried a chill from the water and flowed around her like a playful child.

She moved closer to Sam stealing some of his warmth. She pointed out the features of the houses on the streets as they strolled downhill to the bistro. There were a few Victorians with painted gingerbread edging on the eaves. Two modern buildings that contrasted with the pretty older ones. The rest of the houses, built in the sixties, ranged from boring grey stucco to bright pink clapboard.

"This is the reason I like San Francisco." Sam pointed to the cars parked at an angle on the steep streets. "There aren't any long blocks of treeless sidewalks. The trees make the city like a neighborhood."

"New York is full of neighborhoods," Felicity argued, wrapping her arm around his. "And you have trees."

"Yes, but here there's room to move." He waved his arms to encompass the whole city. "If this was New York it would be people spilling over the sidewalks and taxis filling the streets."

"I suppose, but I'd like to see New York anyway." She leaned her head on his shoulder while they waited for the light to change at the intersection. She hoped the killer was watching, so that he wouldn't be left with any doubts about their relationship. "Shouldn't you be more affectionate?"

"It's supposed to be the first date." Sam gave her arm a squeeze. "Don't go overboard."

"Don't be so stuffy." She giggled. "We have to push him over the edge. We can't do that if you don't play along."

"And we'll lose him if you overdo it." Sam untangled his arm and draped it around her shoulders. "Is this the place?"

Four tables lined the sidewalk, each with two chairs set against the window, so both diners could watch the street. Two people sat at the table farthest from the door, their dinner plates, and wine glasses filling the small round tabletop. A waitress dressed in a white shirt and black pants with a long white apron wrapped around her waist walked to the table.

"Looks like a great place." Sam looked up and down the street. "I think we should sit inside. Then the team can sit outside. We don't want to crowd them too much."

Felicity led Sam inside. "It's a bit too chilly tonight for my taste anyway."

The waitress showed them to a table facing the street and handed them the menus. "Our special today is *osso bucco*; braised veal shank presented on a bed of fingerling potatoes and a ragout of tomatoes and summer squash. Would you like something to drink while you decide?"

"Jamieson's, neat please," Sam ordered.

"Cinzano, on the rocks, please," Felicity added, trying to relax into the evening.

Their server returned to the front of the restaurant after placing their order with the bartender. Felicity watched as the two agents following them were seated at the table outside close to the door. There were no people lurking outside the restaurant and no other diners inside the restaurant. She silently prayed to the Lady to bring this evil man into the open and end this nightmare quickly.

THIRTY-ONE

Sid stood outside Felicity's house and watched the color of the trees on the streets darken as the sun dropped. There was no one home. He'd watched the two leave, his suspicions about Sam confirmed. The casual intimacy of the way they walked together twisted his stomach. They were a couple. It was more important than ever to make very sure that the sacrifice next week was strong enough to break that bond.

He had watched as the two men followed Felicity and Sam to the restaurant and then looked around to see if there was anyone watching the house. There were three cars in the line of sight, and all were empty. There was no one at any of the windows looking onto her side of the street, and no shadows under the other trees, only his.

He fingered the key in his pocket. "It's time," he muttered. "I'm sorry, but I need your essence. I will do penance for this, I swear."

He crossed the street attempting to look confident, like a man returning home after a long day. He ran up the stairs and pulled the key from his pocket sliding it into the lock. Sid turned the key and the doorknob at the same time. The key didn't move.

Ice gripped his stomach and sweat started to form on his hands making the key slippery. Jiggling the key in the lock didn't help. If he couldn't get the door open in the next few seconds, he would have to leave. He couldn't take the chance he would be seen.

Sid closed his eyes and said a prayer, sliding the key out and back into the lock as he whispered. The key turned smoothly. He opened the door and heard the beep of the alarm. He walked over to the panel, tapped four numbers, and the beep stopped. When the Mabon ceremony was complete he would advise his goddess on how to keep such codes secret.

"Fast. Fast, and careful," he muttered. Sid went to the bathroom looking for something with her essence. The counter was bare. "Hurry," he muttered, almost hearing a clock tick as time passed. Opening one of two drawers in the vanity, Sid saw a new toothbrush – still in its wrapper – no good, and some pots of cream which would have too little of her essence to be of use. The second drawer held a tube of toothpaste and a hairbrush. Smiling, Sid pulled four hairs from the brush and carefully laid it back in the drawer.

The hairs went into his jacket pocket, and he looked around as he walked back to the alarm panel. The flower vase was sitting on the coffee table. There were white lilies in the center of the arrangement. He reached in, pinched off the stamens, and held the little orange colored worms of pollen gently in his hand.

"They should have done that at the florist. Sam, Sam, Sam, you should have learned about lilies. They make a big mess with their pollen. Tsk tsk. These will make a great addition to the ground bone, pollen is powerful."

He reached up and pressed the four numbers again, then opened and closed her front door. Sid didn't look around as he locked the door. Whistling quietly, he strode downhill.

THIRTY-TWO

Felicity put down her coffee spoon and sipped her dark roast while Sam munched on the last few bites of the chocolate graham cracker pudding they'd decided to share.

"How long did you live in Italy?" Sam asked.

"Four years." Felicity smiled at the memory of the friends she'd met in those years. "I'm really glad I did it. The experience helped me figure out what I wanted to do. You know, when I was in college I thought I would be an artist or a writer. Then I thought maybe a cook. Being in Italy was a good way to figure out if I wanted to put in the hard work it would take to be good at any of those things. There are fewer distractions when you don't know the language or the people."

Sam signaled for the bill. "I'm glad you came back. Let's go for a walk before we go home. I need to burn off some of that meal."

"Let me pay," Felicity said, reaching for her purse. "You shouldn't have to pay for my plan."

"If he's watching then I need to pay. And I don't remember you asking me out." Sam threw money on top of the receipt. "I pay for dinner when I ask a girl out."

"Sam." Felicity reached to push the money back at him. "I may not have asked you out, but my plan got us here, and I should pay at least half."

Sam shook his head and put the money back on the tray. "Fake date or not, I pay when I take a lady out."

Laughing, Felicity gave up. "Okay, I'll owe you a meal when this is over."

As they left the restaurant, she noticed the two agents pay their bill and leave the table to follow them down to the water.

"Have you ever wanted to do anything other than be an FBI agent?" Felicity cuddled closer to Sam as they walked. The evening chill settled firmly over the city giving her an excuse to cuddle.

"Yes. I did have a different dream at one point. I'm happy as an agent, don't get me wrong." He reached around her shoulders and rubbed her arm.

"But?"

"But I think I would have made a great astronaut."

"Did you try out?" Felicity asked impressed.

"Well they don't usually let five-year-olds fly planes, but I think I'd have done well."

Felicity laughed. "Did you go from astronaut to FBI?"

"Superhero, doctor, race car driver, restaurant owner." Sam counted off the jobs on his fingers. "I did work as a waiter and played in a rock band for a while. I tried out for a baseball team but didn't make it. I drove truck for a summer after college."

"Long way from longshoreman to lawman," Felicity said.

"Yep. I got recruited and it seemed to be the thing I was waiting for. I made it my career."

"What about travel? Have you been anywhere outside the states?"

"No. I'd like to travel but I don't have time." Sam rubbed her arm again. "Are you cold?"

"Yes, how long do we need to walk? Don't get me wrong I'm enjoying it, I just want to warm up."

Sam took off his jacket and laid it across her shoulders. "We can head back, there's no one following us."

"What happens if he doesn't bite?"

"Don't worry about that, it's early. We need to increase the pressure over the next couple of days."

"Telling me not to worry doesn't work, you know."

Sam squeezed her shoulder and kissed the top of her head. A warm glow comforted her at the small intimacies.

They wandered back chatting about trivial subjects. Felicity found herself relaxing and forgetting all the fears and horrors of the last week. Sam was easy to be with, and she didn't want the evening to end. She had to remind herself to keep her feelings safe. It wasn't really a date. It was a trap.

THIRTY-THREE

Sid stepped further back into the shadows as he heard Felicity's laugher float from a block away. The night was quiet and sounds carried through the hush. He could hear Sam's voice but not his words. Whatever the agent was saying made Felicity laugh loudly and return another happy comment. Sid ached to know what they were saying but it was too risky to get closer.

"Enjoy her presence, agent Sam. You'll have that memory to cling to as I draw out your life and energy to the spell." Sid used one hand to rub the lily pollen into the small bag of ground bone in his pocket.

The two walked into sight, arms interlinked, Felicity wrapped in Sam's jacket. The intimacy of their posture was like a knife to Sid's soul. The protective team hung back a block, but Sid could see them. They walked in a state of casual alertness. Looking poised to defend the two lovers against any attack. Sid chuckled. "You won't be able to protect him forever. I'll get him to my circle, don't worry."

The two were at Felicity's front door and for a moment, Sid thought she was going to ask Sam to come in, to spend another night. That would taint the energy of the ceremony. The last night Sam spent in her house was because of work, because she thought she needed him. If she asked him to stay this night, after a date, it would mean they would be sleeping together. Sid would need to cleanse her before they could commune.

"That was fun, thank you," Felicity's voice now carried clearly. "We should do it again, soon."

"How about in the next couple of days?" Sam leaned against the doorframe as he spoke. He reached up and touched the side of her face. "We could play hooky from work and explore the city. I haven't had much of a chance to play the tourist. You could show me what makes San Francisco special."

"I like that idea." Felicity placed her hand on Sam's chest. Sid felt a twist of hatred for Sam. "Figure out what day, and I'll make sure I'm free." She slid her arm around his neck and pulled him in for a kiss.

Sid felt a mix of sickness and pleasure. He could feel the echo of the kiss on his own lips, a tingle that crawled from his mouth to his crotch. He also felt a knife turn in his gut with his jealousy of Sam. "Soon, that will be me," he muttered.

He waited for Sam to walk away, and for the two agents set to protect Felicity to settle in their car, before he edged away from the shadow that hid him. He continued to rub the pollen into the bone as he walked to his home.

THIRTY-FOUR

Sam watched Felicity pick through the barrels of saltwater taffy adding two or three pieces of each flavor to the small basket. This was their second 'date', and he was having a harder time remembering that it was a job not a date. He liked being with her. She knew how to have fun, only he could see the constant strain under the surface.

"You are going to eat some of this, right?" She looked into the basket as she spoke. Sam could see about five pounds of taffy.

"Not that much." He poked at the colored candies. "You can always take it into work."

She stepped closer and whispered, "Anything? Is there any sign he's following us?"

Sam turned her to the cash register. He leaned close and inhaled the scent of her hair before whispering, "Nothing."

Reaching for his wallet, he paid for the saltwater taffy. Felicity handed him a bright yellow candy. He untwisted the wax paper wrapping and tasted lemon. The candy stuck to his teeth as he chewed. Felicity grinned and led him out the door. He wanted to pull her into his arms and give her a lemony kiss, but he knew he couldn't allow himself to believe the lie. He would have to leave her when this case was over and it would be easier if he controlled his feelings.

"Let's go for a drink." She took his arm. "I need to rest my feet. When you said we should take the day off, you didn't mention we'd try to cover the entire city in one go."

"We can stop if you want." Sam hoped she would want to continue. They had gone to Alcatraz first, joking about busman's holidays. The prison on the island stood up to all the hype and seemed to echo with the noise of the inmates who were long gone.

After that, Felicity had led him to the cable car station, and they toured Chinatown, rode over to Van Ness and back to North Beach for Italian food. They'd strolled along the waterfront where Sam tried to push away the memory of Tony's mutilated body from the last time he'd been there.

"No. I'm having too much fun." She took his arm and gave him a quick peck on the cheek.

In the wine bar, she started toward the stools in the window where they would be able to see the street. Sam nudged her. "See if there's a table in the back. We'll let the team following us sit at the window. Maybe if the killer is watching, he'll come in so he can see us."

They ordered two glasses of cabernet sauvignon and an appetizer plate. Sam watched agents Smith and Jones take seats at the front. No one came in after they'd settled.

"Sam." Felicity looked at him over her glass. "I want you to know this last couple of days has been fun. I can't forget about the people who died, but it doesn't feel so overwhelming. I pray for them every night, but you remind me that there is still life for me to live. Thank you for that."

"I'm glad." He cast around for a safer topic. "What should we do next?"

Felicity didn't take the bait. "Have you decided what to do when this is over?"

"I have to go back to New York." He took a sip of the wine to stop himself from asking her to come with him. "There are things I have to deal with there."

"Oh." She looked away from him, gazing at the passing tourists. "Okay."

Sam hoped they were finished with that topic. It was hard enough to keep his feelings under control. He didn't need to discuss them with Felicity. If he took his eye off the job, she might be killed.

"I'll be sorry to see you go," she said.

THIRTY-FIVE

"It's been four days since we started this plan and there's been no action." Sam had called a meeting with Esther, and Detectives Morton and Kang to try to figure out what was going on, or not going on. He needed to make something happen. They couldn't keep pushing and not getting any response.

"You don't know there's been no action," Esther argued. "What he does takes a lot of planning. Just because he hasn't tried to take you yet doesn't mean it's not going to happen today or tomorrow."

"Yes, she's right," Kang added. "If he grabs you too soon what's he going to do with you? He can't take the chance that you'll escape, and he can't keep you drugged for days. He would have to be there to make sure you didn't die."

"I don't like it. It feels like he's still in control, and I think that's a problem." Sam knew Esther was right, but it rankled that he couldn't force the killer to make a move.

"Yes, you do have control issues." Esther winked. "Don't push too hard. This guy is very close to his goal, and he is probably more focused on getting to the end result than you think. If you try to push him over it might backfire."

Bobby Morton stood and walked to the wall of pictures. He looked at them then turned back to the group. "I'm with Sam on this. Well, to the extent that I think we need to push. It doesn't have to be too hard. We just need to raise the stakes a little."

"Thanks." Sam nodded at Bobby, grateful for the support. "I'm not suggesting we make him feel like he's not going to get his way. I just want to push him a bit so he does something that will lower his risk. If he plans to take me tomorrow, then let's make him take me today."

"We don't know if you are the target. Whatever we do could put someone else in danger," Kang said. "What if he's already grabbed his victim?"

"Who?" Sam and Bobby asked at the same time.

"I don't know." Kang shrugged. "Who's left?"

"There's no one left for him to take. We have her staff under observation, and they're fine. We can take them into protective custody, but that might scare the killer off. Her tenant is in Pasadena and the cops there are keeping an eye on him," Bobby said.

"Okay, so what we need is something to make him move today or tomorrow, right?" Kang asked.

"What if you started making more permanent plans with her?" Esther asked. "If he thinks your relationship has progressed to the point where you'll move in, maybe he'll act to stop it."

"Like, what?" Sam asked. "Should I show up with my bags and just move in? It's not like this is a real relationship."

Esther raised her eyebrow.

"What would you normally do in a relationship?"

"It would be moving a bit slower than this. I'd be on date number two, probably. We've been out almost every night since last Saturday." Sam tried not to remember how easy it was to spend time with Felicity.

"So, forget the timeline. What date is this?" Kang asked.

"Four," Sam said. "I guess by now we would have slept together. Date number five is the one that makes or breaks the relationship for me."

"So, does he think you've slept together?" Esther asked.

"Probably not. I leave her at the door with a kiss." Sam tried not to remember the feeling of her lips on his.

Bobby burst out laughing. "Man, no wonder he's not worried. If you aren't getting any, you're no threat. By date number five my wife had me moving in."

Sam held his hands up in surrender. "Okay, I get the point. I'll call her and we'll set up a dirty weekend. If he's looking, or listening, that should make him work fast. We'll plan to take off on Thursday night."

"Thursday morning. You want to make him act and that means tomorrow afternoon at the latest. Otherwise you'll still be on his schedule," Esther said.

"Okay, so where do people go for a dirty weekend around here?" Sam asked.

"Napa," Bobby answered. "Anytime I need to turn on the romance I book a B&B and a nice dinner."

"Yes," Esther added. "Napa is perfect. You might even enjoy it."

They finished planning, and Sam took the names of four bed and breakfasts to call for reservations. He wondered how to get Felicity to agree to a weekend away.

"Be careful how you talk to her about this, if he's watching, he might also be listening," Esther said. "It could be a good idea to stop planning with her and just act."

THIRTY-SIX

Sid watched Felicity's office building from across the street. He leaned against the door of an abandoned store and listened to what happened in her office. The microphone he'd planted last night was picking up the conversation around her desk clearly. He wished he had thought to place one in her home. But if he had, he might have heard them in bed, and he didn't want that memory.

"You are too kind," he muttered when she worked out a solution to one of her employee's problems. "You should sever relationships that don't contribute to your success. It is a pity I have no other sacrifices to make."

Sid twitched his hand in his right pocket, adjusting the volume on the receiver. The sound of the door closing left a vacuum. There was no noise from outside the office, the transmitter only picked up sound for a short distance around her desk.

"Ward, hi, it's Felicity." Sid heard one side of the conversation.

"Thanks, I'm feeling great, and you?"

"I've got good news. I have a temp available to take on your latest manuscript."

"Yes, call her tomorrow after ten and talk over what you need."

"The same number as before. She has the phone."

"Her name is Glenda Wright. Yes, I'm sure you will be happy. Thanks, you too."

Sid heard the phone as she put it in the cradle. "Too kind. Too kind."

He heard her open the door to the office, and then, "Isaac, has Sam called?"

The conversation moved out of range of the microphone. Felicity must have moved to Isaac's desk. He strained and increased the volume, but the words were not audible.

"Okay, thanks." Felicity moved back into the range, her voice hurting his ears until he lowered the volume.

For a few minutes, Sid listened to Felicity open and close drawers and shift paper, then she muttered something he couldn't catch before he heard the tones of a phone being dialed.

"Sam, where are you?" Felicity's voice changed when she talked to Sam, it got warmer. Sid sneered.

He looked up from his feet and saw Sam walking toward the building. "Speak of the devil and the devil appears," he muttered. Sam was talking on his Blackberry. There was no sound from the office as Felicity listened. Then she answered. "That sounds like a good idea. I like the way she thinks. See you in a few minutes."

Sid didn't know what to make of her side of the conversation. He thumbed the volume control on the receiver while he watched Sam enter the building. It was only a minute before the sound of his voice came over the receiver.

"I'm sorry, babe, I should have called earlier." There was a sound of kissing. Sid felt faint with envy.

"What are your big plans?" Felicity sounded breathless.

"You know how we've been trying to get away?"

"Well, yes. You said something about that on the phone, about getting advice to stop planning and start acting."

"Uh huh, I took a chance and acted. Can you play hooky tomorrow, and do you have plans for the weekend?"

"Yes, and no plans that don't include you."

"Okay, pack your bags I've made a reservation for the weekend at Napa Valley B&B. We need to leave tomorrow morning by nine because I've also booked a wine tour."

Sid heard Felicity gasp and the sound of a kiss again. His stomach turned, and panic started to fog his vision. He would need to act fast. He couldn't let them get away for the weekend. There was no way he would be able to bring them back for the Mabon ceremony. He turned off the receiver unable to listen to the two lovers.

As he walked away, Sid muttered options to himself. "Take them before they leave? Take him now? She won't go without him so take him now, or soon. Damn, all the others were easy. This just gets harder and harder."

FELICITY KNEW it was only part of the plan to trap a killer, but she couldn't suppress the excitement she felt about the coming weekend. When she'd phoned him, Sam had carefully avoided referring to a plan. He'd said Esther suggested they take the next step in their relationship. He'd slipped her a note when he was in her office. It read, *we think he's listening so we shouldn't talk about planning anymore.*

"What did Handsome Sam want? He seemed so excited," Isaac asked when he handed her a list of phone calls to return.

"Is there anything new on the slate that needs my attention urgently?" she asked, trying to keep her mind on the fact that it wasn't a real date. Regardless, she just wanted to enjoy her time with Sam, knowing it was short.

"Nothing that can't wait, so far."

"I'm taking tomorrow off, and I won't be available on the weekend." She waited for the inevitable reaction.

"Oh, boss, way to go. You've snapped up a good one there. Handsome and he carries a gun." Isaac rolled his eyes. "How come all the good men are straight?"

"Hah, you don't mean that." Felicity flipped through the messages, most would wait until next week, and the others wouldn't take more than half an hour. "I'll deal with these and then I'll head out unless something else comes up."

Isaac nodded and left her office. Felicity picked up the phone to make the first of four calls. She confirmed that Amanda was available for an urgent assignment on Friday morning. She returned a call to a longtime client who was looking to find a permanent clerk and wanted to know if she knew anyone who might be interested. She left a message with one of the remaining applicants requesting references.

The last call was to return a message regarding another new assignment. It wasn't unusual to have hiccups at the beginning of a relationship, but Felicity was worried that they'd made some mistakes in hiring.

"Hello, Mrs. Garrison. I'm returning your call."

"Oh, yes, Felicity, thanks," Mrs. Garrison's gruff voice responded. "I don't want to cause any problems, but you should know that Joey didn't show up this morning."

"Oh, I'm sorry, did he call?" Felicity felt her tension rise. Was Joey the next victim? Had they failed in their plan?

"No. It's not really a problem as long as he comes tomorrow.

The assignment wasn't urgent." Mrs. Garrison's tone was apologetic. "If you could just let me know he will be here I'm fine."

"I'll check on him, and you'll hear from me, or Isaac, shortly." They ended the call and Felicity immediately called Joey. He didn't answer and she left a message for him with her cell number.

"Isaac, do you know how to get hold of Joey?" she called.

"I've got a personal cell number. Why?" He stood in her doorway. "Is there a problem?"

"Let me have it. He didn't show up for his assignment."

"Oh no, you don't think he's a victim, do you?"

"No, don't think that. It's probably just a normal problem." She called the number and left another message.

Then she called Sam and let him know the details of the missing temp, keeping in mind the killer might be listening. "I'm worried. Do you think it's possible he's the latest victim?"

"I hope not. Let me get some feelers out and I'll get back to you." Sam ended the call.

"Isaac, I'm going home. I've done all I can think of to find Joey. Go on home yourself. I'll leave you a message before I head out for the weekend. Someone will call you when they find out about Joey."

THIRTY-SEVEN

Sid was still standing outside her office as she left. He watched Felicity get into the black sedan waiting in front of the building.

He worried that the protection team would get in the way of his plans. He knew they would stay with Felicity, so grabbing Sam wouldn't be a problem. The problem he saw was bringing Felicity to the ceremony on Friday. They wouldn't let her out of their sight, and they wouldn't be easy to distract.

Tonight, Sid decided. He would take Sam tonight and put him under to hold him quiet for a day. Later when the two men watching her house would be tired, he would try getting in the back of her home. It was out of their line of sight, and unless they walked around the building, he could get in and see what the opportunities were. He could drug her and carry her out the back. Yes, that would solve his problem. No one would be looking for her, except Sam and the protection team. Sam would be out of action the protection team could only look for her. They would have no way to track her down.

The important thing would be to make sure he followed Sam home. He needed to get in place now, so they didn't slip out without him seeing them. It would be okay if they went out for a date, well okay to his plan not okay to his feelings. But if they decided to leave a day early for their weekend, it would be a disaster.

SAM OPENED the door for Felicity and handed her keys back to her. They had eaten pizza and walked along the waterfront until dark. Her hands were full of bags from last minute grocery shopping.

"I'll be by at eight and we can get started," he said as she went through the door.

Sid grinned in the shadows across the street. "Plans have changed don't waste your time getting ready."

He glanced at the car across from him. Tonight, it was a black SUV with tinted windows and chrome details. Sid smiled. Hard to tell if they were agents or drug dealers. While he watched from the safety of his cover, two men stepped out of the vehicle and crossed the street to enter the house. That meant they wouldn't be watching when Sam left.

Sid said a small prayer of thanks that Sam had walked not driven to her house. It would be easy to follow him, and easy to take him when they got to the first quiet place.

"See you tomorrow." Sam's voice carried across the quiet street. He strode down the steps and headed downhill.

Sid waited until Sam was half way down the block before stepping out of the shadow and strolling down the same street, always a half block away. He walked close to the buildings, prepared to step into a doorway if Sam seemed suspicious. His focus lay only on the broad shoulders of the man walking ahead of him.

The sound of Sam's phone ringing floated back to Sid in the quiet of the night. "Okay," he responded to whoever was on the phone. "How far? Okay." Sam clicked the phone shut.

Sid's skin began to crawl. He stopped and checked his watch as if he was late for an appointment. He looked back from where he was standing and saw no one. He coughed into his shoulder and looked in the other direction. There was no one there either. He put aside his fears that they had somehow seen him and started after Sam again. Sid turned, faced downhill, and gasped. Sam was gone. He'd lost him. He would have to change his plan. Somehow, he would have to take Sam tomorrow.

"Don't despair. The harder the task she sets the more worthwhile the reward," he muttered.

THIRTY-EIGHT

Agent Smith stepped out of the doorway as the target started to walk quickly down the street. He smiled. *Gotcha you bastard.* The plan had been brilliant. Esther suggested that if they were right, and the killer was watching her house, then he'd probably seen the team come and go. It worked for her protection, but protection wasn't the only goal. They wanted to catch him too.

Smith had been there when she'd suggested the change, three men, tinted windows. He agreed with the assessment. The idea was if the killer were watching them, he'd see the two men enter Felicity's house and think he was safe. It had worked like salt on ice. Now he was following the serial killer to find the evidence to link him to this horrible crime spree. There would be no thirteenth victim.

Hanging back a block, Smith followed the target downhill until they entered a busier section of town. The killer didn't seem to notice the tail, he was so fixated on moving through the streets. They turned onto Market Street and the noise and crowds of tourists allowed the agent to move closer without drawing attention. The sound of jazz blared out of a bar on the corner of Post and Market. The honk of car horns and laughter of the happy drunks flowed over him as he dodged people to keep the killer in his line of sight.

His BlackBerry vibrated and when he flipped it open, there was a text message from the other two agents. *On market, on foot, where to go?* He texted back, *at Geary, black jacket, black ball cap, hunched over, 6 feet, heavy*. There were better odds of staying with him now. Three agents could make sure that they never lost the target. Even if he caught one, the other two could keep the tail on.

On him, see me? Smith looked at the people around the killer. Agent Jones was standing in the doorway of DSW staring at the killer's back. *Yes, stay on him. I'll update.* Smith continued to follow but eased his focus enough to dial Sam's number.

"We're on him. I'll let you know when he stops. What's going on there?"

"Nothing, she's settling in for the night. I think it's a relief we've found him," Sam said. "I'll stay here until we get someone to replace me. Until we are one hundred percent, I don't want to leave her alone."

"Yeah. I know what you mean. It's going almost too smoothly. I'll call you with an address as soon as he goes inside somewhere. Do you have a judge lined up for the warrant?"

"I've got someone on it. Keep alert." Sam hung up.

Agent Smith watched as their target turned on Columbus and headed south of Market. "Damn, is he heading for her office?" This wasn't going to work if he just stood outside her office until morning.

He called the other two agents and gave the signal to be alert – letting the phone vibrate once before he hung up. With the crowds thinning, they needed to be very careful. Now they were moving out of the tourist areas, it would be easy for the killer to notice the three agents following as he approached his destination.

Smith pulled into a doorway and waited for the other agents to pass. Jones passed first. "Go around the block," Smith said quietly. Agent Jones walked the ten steps to the end of the block and turned right. Agent Simons passed a minute later. "Go left," Smith whispered as she passed. The blonde agent walked to the end of the block and looked at the street sign. She took a small piece of paper out of her pocket and checked as though she was looking for an address. She looked left and right as though checking the numbers on the door, then nodded and turned to cross the street and walk quickly down the opposite direction to agent Jones.

Smith knew the other two agents would quickly round the blocks and join him unless he sent a signal to stay. Smith stepped out of the doorway and walked straight down the road, the killer was two blocks away. Felicity's office was one block ahead of him on the right.

The killer walked through a pool of light and past the office with a glance upward. Smith sighed in relief and sped up slightly. It looked like they would find out where this maniac hung out.

Twenty minutes later, Smith stood in another doorway and watched the killer open the door to a warehouse on Industrial Street. It felt like he'd aged ten years during the time it took to get from Felicity's house to this place. There was a car repair shop on one side and a distribution center on the other. The warehouse was set in the middle of a lot and protected by a chain link fence, a perfect place for private activities that might make a lot of noise.

Smith buzzed the other two agents twice, the signal to draw back. Then he made the call to Sam.

THIRTY-NINE

"Why are we still waiting?" Felicity paced through her apartment. "You know where he's committing these crimes, and we're just sitting here."

"Yes," Sam agreed. "And we'll just sit here until I get the call that we have a warrant."

"How long is that going to take?"

"It usually takes a while, but don't worry so much. We're watching him and he's still in the warehouse."

"But it's the day before Mabon. He has to act soon. And we're supposed to be going away. If he's hiding in his warehouse, how do you think he's planning to get you? To get us?"

"I don't know, but it doesn't matter." Sam stood and walked to the window. "There's no way for him to get out. We have agents watching the entire perimeter of the building. He will be there when we arrive."

"Why don't we go down there and wait for the warrant?" She knew Sam wanted keep her safe in her home as long as he could, but couldn't stop asking questions.

"When I said we, I meant the FBI. You are staying home and someone will be here just in case." Sam turned away.

"No, I'm coming." Felicity spun around to face him.

"No, you aren't." Sam crossed his arms over his chest. "You'll just get in the way."

"You can't stop me. I'm not under arrest, and I can go where I want." She stamped her foot. "Great, now you've pushed me into being a two-year-old. Thanks a lot."

Sam choked down a laugh. "It really is too dangerous. Why won't you stay and make it easy for everyone?"

"I have a feeling. Don't you dare laugh, I mean it." She shook her head in frustration. "I really do have this feeling like a burning in my bones. I have to be there."

"Will you do everything we tell you?" Sam asked.

"If I can," Felicity said, happy he was relenting.

"I need more than that. If we tell you to stay put, you need to do that. If you don't, it means everyone is in danger." Sam looked carefully at her face as she considered. "Well?"

"Okay, I don't want anyone else hurt, but I need to be there." She didn't say that she didn't want Sam out of her sight. He was the only one she cared about being in danger.

Sam's phone rang. "Barton. Yes, I'm on my way." He closed the phone and looked at Felicity. "The warrant has been signed, and they are on the way to the warehouse. Get your coat, it's time to go."

FORTY

Felicity saw six agents waiting beside the van.

Agent Smith held up the warrant and nodded.

"He hasn't come out." Smith confirmed. "I guess we should cut the chain on the gate and go knock on the door."

The agents checked their guns and pulled the straps of their bulletproof vests tight. "Felicity, stay here in the van with the doors locked until we make sure he's not able to get away," Sam ordered.

"Yes, Sir." She saluted. "Don't forget to come and get me or I'll follow you in, I swear."

"Don't be a smartass."

The agents left at a run. Simons used the bolt cutters to snap the chain holding the gate closed. Felicity watched as they ran up to the warehouse door and stood on each side. Sam knocked loudly on the door and called out for someone to open it. After a minute, he hammered his fist on the door again and repeated his request.

She watched him nod at the two agents holding a battering ram. They stood back and swung the weighted metal against the door, once, twice, three times. The door swung open, and two agents ran inside, ducking and turning different directions as they entered. The rest of the agents went in and then there was nothing to watch. Felicity waited what seemed to be an age before Sam came back out. He strode to the van and opened the door.

"He's not there." Sam rolled his shoulders. "It's weird. You might be able to help us figure out what's going on." He handed her a set of latex gloves. "Here put these on, and make sure you don't touch anything without them."

She was glad to be useful at last. "Okay. I never asked, but do we know who he is?"

"The warehouse is owned by a Sidney Parker. We did some research last night He's what we call a ghost. There's no record of him committing any crimes. He doesn't have a driver's license, nor has he been in the armed forces."

"You think this Sidney is the killer?"

Sam gestured to the dark interior of the warehouse. "We're working under that assumption. There's no record of a lease to anyone else, so we only have Mr. Parker to go on. A team went to the residence listed on the ownership papers and there's an old, run down house. No one was home. We checked with the neighbors and they say a guy lives there alone, about mid-thirties, red hair, pasty skin, loner."

The air in the warehouse was damp. Felicity couldn't quite recognize the smell, metallic and sharp at the same time. It caught in the back of her throat and she coughed. "That looks like a pentagram." She pointed to half brushed away lines in a white powder. "It might be where he killed those poor people."

"There's more in this room in the back." Sam led her to a room that looked like an office.

"Agent Barton," Simons called before they could enter the office. "We've cleared the upstairs visually. There's no one there, do you want us to get dogs in?"

"No, if the place is empty then let's not contaminate anything with the dogs. You head over to the house with everyone else. I'll call the crime scene team when we've looked through this stuff."

Simons nodded and signaled to the other agents to leave.

Sam turned back to see Felicity flipping through a book. Leaning over her, he asked, "Can you make any sense of that? Some of it doesn't seem to be in English."

"It's not. It's an old form of Celtic script. Some Wiccans follow a path that uses Celtic symbols and words." She pointed to a symbol drawn in the center of one page. "This is a charm. It is used for protection during rites."

"Any particular rites?" Sam asked.

"No, it's part of every rite. It protects the priest while he or she is filled with the spirit of the God or Goddess." She flipped a page. The silence of the building was chilling her to the bone. "What's in that cupboard?" She pointed to a wall-mounted cupboard next to the door to a closet.

"Some powders and candles." He reached over and tugged at the door handle. "There's a knife wrapped in velvet."

"His anthame. The knife he uses for rituals," she said.

"We'll test it for blood."

"You might not find anything. He will have cleaned it thoroughly with bleach to remove the energy of the rite. After that, he would have oiled it to protect the blade."

"It's worth a try anyway. You said he doesn't follow a path you recognize; did I say that right?"

"Yes. I don't see anything that would form a pattern of any path. Here are colored candles. We use them for ceremonies, but the symbols carved into the wax are like nothing I've seen before." She picked up a white candle and pointed to the stars.

She pulled out jars of powders and liquids and placed them on the table. When they were all out of the cupboard, she opened and sniffed at some of them. "Mustard, fennel, vinegar," she said putting each vial aside as she identified it. "I don't know what this white powder is, but this is sand."

"We'll check all the contents in the lab, don't keep trying them. There might be something poisonous there." Sam opened the door to the closet. "Would he need special clothes?"

Felicity nodded, reaching in to pull out the robes. "He would need this for Beltane." She handed Sam a white robe that he put on the table. "Here's the one he would need for tomorrow." She passed him a black robe.

"How many robes would he need?"

"Depending on what he celebrates, he might need twelve. There aren't that many here." She moved the robes to one side. "Sam, there's another door back here."

"Get back." He pulled her roughly into the room. "How the hell did the team miss this? I'll check it out. You stay here, okay?"

"Yes, I'll stay back. Be careful, Sam." Felicity moved close to the door, whispering a prayer for protection.

Sam pulled out his gun and flicked off the safety. He moved aside the remaining robes to look at the door. Metal with a handle, but no lock. "It might just be a service door," he called back to her.

Sam opened the door and stepped back in case someone came through. Felicity saw him pull a small flashlight from his pocket and shine its light into the doorway.

"It does look like a service room," Sam said. "It's more like a corridor than a room."

Felicity realized she was holding her breath, and let it out slowly, trying to release all the tension from the last days.

It was over.

"You can come in." Sam came into the office and beckoned Felicity. "Check this out."

She followed him into the room. "I don't think this has any ceremonial meaning, you're right, it is more like a corridor."

"Do you know what these are?" Sam shone the flashlight over the brick wall.

She looked over Sam's shoulder at the bareness of the room. "Those are runes." Moving closer to the wall, Felicity nudged Sam behind her. "This one that looks like a malformed capital F, it's the sign for a god force. This one that looks like a weird capital P is the sign for breaking resistance."

Felicity heard a clicking noise, and turned to see a man standing behind Sam. Before she could scream, he pointed something at Sam and shot.

Sam folded at the knees and fell jerking to the floor.

The man smiled at her and nodded as if respecting her. He slammed the door locking her inside.

She screamed.

Bending, she touched Sam's neck, fearing that he was dead. Relief overwhelmed her as his pulse twitched under her finger.

"Lord and Lady protect me from this madness. Protect my friend and any others that come within the sway of this broken soul who has done these deeds in your name." She breathed her prayer, eyes closed, as she sank to the floor and kept her hand on Sam's unconscious body.

FORTY-ONE

Sid giggled. He had Sam trapped. Everything would work out. The agents searching his warehouse had missed the hidden room upstairs, a match to this one and accessed from the back of the janitor's closet. The Lord and Lady were smiling on him today. His plans would come to fruition perfectly.

He ignored the scream from Felicity. She would understand after he was done. Sam had blinded her to the truth. When his life force fled, she would see.

He needed to keep them quiet for a few hours while he prepared. From a bag on the table, he pulled a small canister with a spray nozzle on top. Sid put on latex gloves and a paper mask for protection. He had done a lot of research to find the best way to render them unconscious until the ceremony.

The canister he held was from a veterinarian's office. He only needed to spray a small amount into the room. In a couple of minutes, both of them would be asleep. That would hold them long enough for him to do what he needed to do.

Sid went back through the closet and bent to slide the nozzle into the crack between the floor and door. He counted to twenty while he sprayed. He heard Felicity cough, then no sound. Sid counted to thirty then held his breath and opened the door. They were both unconscious. He drew back and left the door open for one minute to let the vapor disperse.

He kept his mask on and went into the cramped space to take their BlackBerrys and a second phone he found on Sam.

He placed Felicity in a more comfortable position. She would need to be unconscious for a long time, and he didn't want her to suffer from any aches or bruises because he'd left her lying in an awkward position. Slipping a cushion under her neck, he draped an old robe over her.

Sam he didn't worry about. Sid roughly rolled him over and jabbed Sam's buttocks with a small disposable hypodermic needle. More loot from the veterinarian's office. He took a second needle and gently slid it under Felicity's skin.

"Sleep well, my goddess," he murmured, patting the skin he had just penetrated. "You will wake to a better place, and we will live in glorious love."

Sid returned to the office and placed the phones and PDAs on the table. He picked up Sam's BlackBerry and pressed the on button. The screen read, enter password. In a rage, Sid threw it against the wall. It shattered. He picked up Felicity's and was able to access the contact list and email without a password. He placed it to one side. Unlike his BlackBerry, Sam's phone started without a password. Sid checked the address book and found Simons. He knew that was one of the agents because he had been able to hear the searchers talking.

"What should I say?" Sid tapped his lips with a finger then scrolled through the phone's menu. "Ah, texting is an excellent idea."

He mulled over the content he was going to send and then started typing. *Team is here. Nothing coming up. Stay there until he shows. We're heading out per original plans.* That should buy him a day while the rest of the investigators waited for further instructions.

"Lord and Lady, I beg you to add your power to this message, to make them believe," he whispered as he pressed the send key.

Sid turned off the phone, picked up Felicity's PDA, pulled Isaac's email out of the address book. He chose email contact from the list of tasks available then typed, *off to Napa with Sam. Have a great weekend. See you Monday.* He turned off her BlackBerry.

FORTY-TWO

Sid smiled at his work. He'd spent the day and night purifying himself for the ceremony. In the moments between cleansing and punishing himself, he had checked on his captives. Agent Sam was almost conscious the last time he'd looked. Jamming another small dose of anesthetic into the agent, he checked on Felicity. He worried that too much drug would cause her damage and was glad to find her still deeply unconscious. He hadn't planned for both of them to need drugging, or for Agent Barton to be a day early. There were still enough drugs to give a second shot to Felicity, but if Sam came around again too early, he would have a problem. Sid decided to hold back just in case Sam came to. He sent another text to the FBI agents. No one seemed to question the delay.

Sid took his knife and drew his own blood to make a sacrifice of life force. This was the last cleansing ritual. His wait was almost over. Midnight had come and gone an hour ago, and Sid could feel the forces of power swirl around and grow stronger. "Lord and Lady, I feel your presence, I feel the changes coming."

He picked up the pail of water from the stool bedside his

mat. The ice rattled against the metal side of the pail as he raised it and poured it over his head. He gasped as the cold went through to his bones. The last step of cleansing his flesh bit through the cuts he had whipped into his back.

He dried himself with a rough white towel, wincing as the coarse fabric reopened his cuts. When he was dry, Sid picked up a jug of oil that was warming on a heating pad. He dipped his index finger into the oil to check the temperature, then he poured some into his palm and spread it over his body. Sid continued this motion slowly massaging in the oil until he was covered in a slick sheen, and he smelled the faint scent of lavender and sage.

The electronic timer chimed three times, paused, and chimed again. He pressed the button to stop the noise. Sid looked around at the simple equipment he had gathered to help him reach this sense of peace and readiness. It was time to start the preparations for the ceremony downstairs. Time to draw the circle and call the powers to finish the joining of his earthly body to her holy being. He cleared the small circle careful to pick up all the items before stepping out. He didn't want to disturb the spirits who were already gathered.

After placing the items in the credenza, Sid slowly walked out of the office and locked the door. He walked in a measured pace down the hallway to the stairs leading to the warehouse. He unlocked the door to the warehouse and stepped through. His heart was beating slowly, and he focused on keeping it that way. He needed to be centered for the Mabon rites.

The floor of the warehouse was clean. In the exact center of the east wall, stood the table holding the equipment he needed. Sid took the robe that lay folded on the end of the table and dropped it over his head. The last hypodermic lay beside the anthame and the pots of powder. He picked it up and walked through the office door. Sid placed his ear on the door to the temporary prison. There was no sound. Afraid of a trap, he looked around for something to help defend himself in case Sam was awake. The dose should keep him unconscious for another hour, enough time to complete the ceremony, but it wasn't easy to judge the effects on a man. He had put the Taser on the desk earlier so he could stun Sam if needed. He picked it up and thumbed it into active mode. The clicking irritated his calm state, but that was better than having Sam attack.

He opened the door a crack, Sam was on the floor in the same position Sid had left him. Felicity still lay on her side as though she was sleeping, her body rising and falling gently with her breath. Sid kicked Sam and there was no reaction. He was out cold. Sid smiled.

Sam's body was heavy as Sid dragged him to the center of the room dropping him on his back. Sid took the anthame and cut Sam's shirt open. Then he sprinkled a trace of ground bone on Sam's chest. When his fingers were clean of bone, Sid went to the table and took some paste made of lemon and rosemary and smeared that into to the ground bone powder.

"Sam," Felicity's voice cracked and wavered. "Sam, where are you?"

Sid looked to see if there was any reaction from Sam, none. He ran on tiptoes to the office, she was still there, in the back room. He sidled into the room and crouched down beside her. "Sam is not here. You'll see him soon." He reached out to touch her but pulled back when she winced.

"Where is he, what are you doing to him?" She seemed to force the words through her throat.

"Only what he deserves. Don't worry it will soon be done." Sid pushed some of the drug out of the hypodermic he held behind his back. "Hush, be quiet now."

"No, I won't be quiet." She tried to hit him, but she didn't have any control over her arms. She missed, grazing her knuckles on the rough wall.

"Take care, my lady." Sid held her hand and placed his lips on the grazes. "I thank you for the gift of your essence."

She pulled her hand away. "Don't touch me."

"I hope and pray you will forgive me for this." Sid held her arm in one hand and checked to make sure he had expelled more than half of the liquid in the vial, then plunged the needle into the muscle on her upper arm.

"No, don't." Felicity struggled for a minute before her eyes closed and she slumped into unconsciousness.

SID TOOK the bowl of bone powder and pollen that he'd mixed to bring the strength of death and life together. There was still too little to make the full circle big enough to hold Sam and let Sid write the runes. He took a bag of kosher salt and a mortar and pestle. He placed the bone and pollen mix and a handful of the salt in the bowl and ground them together breaking the salt into smaller fragments. Checking the amounts, Sid added another handful of salt into the mixture.

He walked back to Sam's body and placed the bowl of salt and bone at his head. Sid brought the oil and lantern and placed them beside Sam's right hand. He took the wine, placed it at the agent's feet, and then placed the incense at Sam's left hand.

It was time to bring Felicity out. The ceremony required her to be there when the climax came. Sid went to the back room and bent beside her sleeping form. He placed one arm beneath her knees and the other under her shoulders. He grunted as he lifted her; dead weight was dead weight.

Ignoring the twinge from his lower back, Sid lay her gently down, and kissed her forehead. Before he moved away, he double-checked she wouldn't be too close to the circle. "Perfect." He kissed her again and then moved away.

It was time to call the quarters to start the ceremony. Sid stepped to Sam's head and faced down with his eyes closed. He raised his arms to shoulder height and then brought them together palms facing in front of his body. Sid raised his head and opened his eyes.

He pulled a bundle of sage from the pocket of his robe and lit it with a disposable lighter. He waved the smoke in vertical circles over the body in the center, and then around the area where he would draw his circle. Then he passed the bundle over Felicity, and finally over his own body. "I bless this place and cleanse it in the name of the Goddess."

He placed the burning sage on the floor away from the circle, then returned to the beginning. Sid bent and picked up the bowl of bone mixture. Walking counter clockwise sprinkling a line of the slightly yellowed powder, Sid hummed tunelessly and constantly. He made sure to include all of the ingredients of the spells inside the circle as he moved, there wasn't enough to break and heal the circle if he forgot something.

When the circle was complete, he bent and picked up the anthame. He looked up and pointed the knife down. "Spirit of the East, Ancient One of the Air, I ask you to join with me. Be with me and guard me in my circle. Blessed be, Spirit."

Sid turned and walked clockwise to the south. "Spirit of the South, Ancient One of Fire, I ask you to join with me. Be with me and guard me in my circle. Blessed be, Spirit." Sid continued clockwise to the west. "Spirit of the West, Ancient One of Water, I ask you to join with me. Be with me and guard me in my circle. Blessed be, Spirit." And then to the north. "Spirit of the North, Ancient One of the Earth, I ask you to join with me. Be with me and guard me in my circle. Blessed be, Spirit."

Sid stood again at the east and Sam's head.

FORTY-THREE

Felicity heard Sid calling the quarters before she could open her eyes. Consciousness returned to her mind before it returned to her body. He had finished calling North, when she was able to open her eyes and roll her head toward the sound, and the sight of Sam's body in the center of the circle.

"Now, I consecrate the holy circle with this oil steeped with rosemary for remembrance and lemon for purity."

She watched Sid pace counterclockwise with a jar of oil in his right hand. It looked like he was drawing a second circle just inside the first. She could smell sage smoke overlaid with the astringency of the rosemary and the sweet tartness of the lemon. Sid's back was to her and Felicity felt a tingling in her arms and legs. She tried to turn over before he could see her move. It worked and she could now watch the progress of the ceremony without strain on her neck.

Sam was in one piece. She couldn't see any blood on his clothes or face, so the rite couldn't have been too far along. She felt tears seep from the corners of her eyes in mourning of Sam's death.

Sid finished the oil circle and placed the pot down inside.

He picked up a red candle and lit it with a disposable lighter. Felicity could feel the floor against her body now. She knew that it would be difficult if she needed to stand and run, but her most critical fear was having Sid see that she had moved. He was standing at the next quarter and lighting a white candle. It was too late to move back. She closed her eyes and pretended to be unconscious. Sending a quiet prayer for rescue.

Sid's shuffling steps moved past her without pausing. She waited until he passed before she opened her eyes. A yellow candle stood in her line of sight, the flame barely moving in the still air of the warehouse. She stared past the flame to Sam and held her breath as she saw his chest rise and fall. He was alive! She scanned the room as far as she could without moving her head. The only thing in sight that would work as a weapon was the candle. She watched as Sid lit the wick of the final one, black.

Sid started to cense the circle with pine incense. This time he would pass in front of her as he started the circle. She slid her arm out and wiggled her fingers to hurry the circulation back. As Sid passed, she flicked her hand out and tipped the candle into the oil circle.

The flame hit the oil and started to run around the circle as though the guardians were putting up their power to block out her entry.

Sid spun around, his robe swinging and catching the flame. The flimsy fabric caught fire quickly. He screamed in surprise, and spun back around dropping the incense sticks, and trying to pat out the flames on the fabric. His frantic activity gave Felicity a chance to struggle to her feet. She needed to get Sam out of the circle before Sid recovered.

Standing made her head spin, so she stumbled only half upright into the circle. She would normally never think to enter another Wiccan's circle, but Sid wasn't a Wiccan, and his circle wasn't sacred.

The flames were going out in the area around Sam's feet, so she headed for there and grabbed hold of his ankles. Bending her knees and planting her feet, Felicity fell backward to pull Sam a few feet away from the center. She struggled back to her feet and found her balance a little better this time. She managed to pull Sam all the way out and into safety as he started coughing.

"No," Sid screamed. "Why are you doing that? Stop. The spell will not work now." He rushed toward Sam's body and tripped over a torn fragment of his robe. As he fell, he knocked over the oil jar, shattering it. Oil splattered on his robes, covering him from hem to neckline in large drops. He rolled as he landed and brushed the red candle with his arm. The flame licked his skin. Consuming oil, hair, clothes, and skin before Sid could react.

"Oh, Lord and Lady." Felicity shuddered and closed her eyes as Sid's robe went up in a flash of blue flame. She looked for something to cover the fire, but her legs wouldn't coordinate. She collapsed on the second step.

Sid screamed. His voice trailing out into a whimper. As she watched helpless, she saw him inhale flame, his eyes widening, the expression agony, or rapture. Felicity whispered a prayer to Brigid the aspect of fire to lead him from this world. "No one should suffer this death," she muttered as she tried to force her still weak body to move.

The reek of charred flesh added to the heavy smells from the rite. Felicity covered her mouth, stifled the coughing fit she felt coming on, and started to crawl toward the office. She needed to call for help and hoped there was a phone there, one that was hooked up to service.

In the office, she found her BlackBerry on the table. It felt like an eternity before it powered up so she could dial. The 911 operator answered immediately. "Please we need help. There's a fire. A man is dead. I don't know the exact address. It's a warehouse on Industrial Street. I think the cross street is Revere. I need help for Agent Barton. If I can get out, I'll wait and wave to the ambulance." The coughing fit came back, and she couldn't hold it down anymore.

"Ma'am, stay on the phone, someone should be there in two minutes."

"Thanks," Felicity gasped. The operator kept speaking to her as Felicity returned to Sam.

He was struggling to sit up.

The flames were dead, but Sid's body still smoldered, wisps of smoke curling from him into the already hazy air.

FORTY-FOUR

Bobby Morton stood outside the warehouse. He could see scorch marks on the floor inside, and the smell of burned wood was tainted with the odor of charred flesh.

A firefighter walked out of the building with the half strut, half trudge they had. Strut of a hero, trudge of someone carrying a heavy weight. Bobby went over and showed his badge. "Bobby Morton, how's it going?"

"Pete Wilson." He held out a gloved hand and shook Bobby's offered one. "We're done."

"Can we go in?" Bobby asked. "We need to close off the details. We've also got four more bodies to find. God knows, we want to make sure we have all the victims accounted for."

"Go ahead." Pete nodded toward the door. "There are no more combustibles. It's safe. The guy had a ton of weird things though."

"Yeah. Weird guys collect weird things," Bobby agreed.

"You said you were looking for more bodies?" Pete asked. "The dogs were nosing around the back for a while. There's a patch of garden back there. I guess the designers were looking to make it a bit nicer here for the workers. Anyway, you might want to check it out."

"Did the dogs find anything else?" Bobby was curious how Sid had hidden from the FBI when they searched the building.

"Three hidden rooms. Two upstairs and the one the FBI agent found. The guy spent time in each one. The dogs had trouble with the one downstairs, I think the smells of what he was doing there covered his scent. If the dogs had trouble, you would have needed a lot of luck to find it." Peter turned away and started to return to the truck. "Good luck."

"Thanks," Bobby called back. "I'm going to need it, I think."

He walked around the back of the building and saw the patch of garden that the fireman mentioned. The dirt didn't seem like it had been freshly dug. Most of it was covered with new sod. The sod was browning in patches. Bobby assumed it was due to lack of care. There was a patch of the garden planted with greenery. It looked innocent and homey, like his grandmother's herb garden.

Pulling his phone out of his pocket, Bobby called into the station to get a team to dig up the dirt. His second call was to Agent Simons to let her know the building was clear. Simons said she would be right there, and not to touch anything.

Ten minutes later Agent Simons showed up with two other agents in tow. As they parked the black SUV, the police team pulled up with shovels in hand.

"What's that for?" Simons asked tilting her head toward the van.

"We might have found the other bodies." Bobby instructed the four men to start digging up the garden patch. "How's agent Barton?"

"He's bullying the nurses and doctors into releasing him," Jones said. "I don't doubt he'll show up here before you know it."

"And Ms. Armstrong?"

"She was in a pretty bad state. They checked her into the hospital overnight, but she calmed down enough to go home this morning. She's not hurt, just badly shaken up. They gave her some sedatives, or something. I'm guessing it will take a while before she feels the impact. I've seen people suddenly break down months after this kind of trauma."

"Is anyone with her?"

"No. Her assistant picked her up. But she should be safe, why?"

"Turn around." Bobby pointed. Felicity was getting out of a taxi across the street. "It might have helped to keep her at home."

"Morton. Hey, Morton." One of the police officers came around the building. "Come on back here."

FELICITY STOOD DEBATING whether to follow them or wait for Sam. He'd called and told her to meet him here. She decided to follow. "Face your fears. Don't let that killer make you change your life."

"Hold up," Sam called as he stepped out of a second cab. "What's going on?"

"I don't know." She took his arm and they started to walk around the building. "Detective Morton seems to have found something out back. Are you sure you are okay?"

"Yes, don't fuss. I've got a bit of a headache, but nothing permanent is wrong." He winced as he spoke.

Simons turned away from the group and walked over to Sam and Felicity. "They peeled back the sod and found bodies, four of them, two men two women."

"Yeah. We have notes we couldn't match to bodies. That seems to fit," Sam agreed. "Good work."

Felicity drew Sam away from the burials. "Let them deal with this. It's over."

FORTY-FIVE

Felicity returned to work on the Monday after the fire, trying to get back to normal as quickly as possible. It had been a mixed success. She valued the routine but found it difficult to keep her concentration for more than a half hour at a time. She would come out of a daze and find twenty minutes passed without her knowing.

Isaac opened her door and caught her staring off into space. "Sam's here, do you want me to send him in?"

Felicity brought her attention back to the moment. "Yes, please."

Sam walked in looking fresh and full of life. He looked at Felicity. "You look like crap. Sorry, that was rude."

"No, it was honest." She smiled. Heat rising at the memory of the kisses they'd shared.

He sat across from her. "Have you talked to Victims Services yet?"

"No, I haven't been able to find time. I'll be okay, don't worry." She hoped it was true, this deadness inside wasn't right. She should feel something.

"No, you won't be okay, believe me. You need to talk to

someone with training to help people get past this kind of stuff. Most people have friends to support them. Sid Parker took them from you." He held her hand. "Are you getting any sleep?"

"Not much. I keep seeing his body go up in flames." She shuddered. "I feel responsible for his death. I know he killed so many people, all my friends, but I killed him. I tipped over the candle."

"No, you aren't responsible."

"There didn't seem to be a reason he lit up that way, there wasn't enough oil on the ground to cause such a lot of damage."

"It wasn't on the ground. He was covered in oil. It looked like he'd rubbed it all over his body." Sam squeezed her hand. "He did this to himself."

"The threefold rule." She sighed. "He suffered for all the damage he did."

"You still didn't cause it." He sounded worried. "If you're right, then you were just the agent of his punishment."

"I know. And I pray for him to be forgiven." She shook her head. "I'm sure I'll be fine. It's only been two days, Sam. I think there would be something seriously wrong with me if I just snapped back after that."

He drew back from her. "People react differently."

"I don't mean you should be a mess too. Oh, Sam, you have all kinds of training. I mean you help people like me, civilians."

"I know you didn't mean anything by it." Sam rose and wrapped his arms around her shoulders kissing the top of her head.

Felicity leaned into his embrace, feeling the warmth of his body give her strength.

"It was nice. The dating, I mean," she murmured.

"It was." He kissed her cheek. "It was supposed to be part of the job."

"I know, but it didn't feel like a job." She looked up at him. "I thought maybe there was something else happening."

"Definitely something else." He kissed her.

Felicity felt the fear and horror of the last few days drain away with the passion. When the kiss ended, she pulled away. "You came here, and I don't think it was to kiss me, or not just to kiss me." She knew he wouldn't stay. That whatever was happening between them wouldn't be strong enough for him to stay. His life was in New York.

"I'm heading back to New York tomorrow." He gave her a squeeze. "Come with me, take a vacation, and spend a week just recovering."

"A week?" Felicity asked.

"For a start." He smiled. "Let's see what happens after a week."

"Are you going to take the week as a vacation? Or are you going to work?"

"I have a few issues I need to deal with, but they can wait a week." Sam lifted Felicity's chin. "I'm going to fix those problems so I can put in for a transfer."

"A transfer?" She smiled. "Here?"

"If you think I would be welcome."

She pulled him toward her. "I think you'll be very welcome."

WANT MORE?

More drama, more thrills. Use the QR code to get your copy of the next City Crimes books, THE DRAGON AT THE EDGE OF THE MAP

Sneak peek on the next page.

If you enjoyed reading Closing the Circle, please consider helping other readers to find the story by leaving a review.

CHAPTER 1

Monique climbed the last set of stairs to her fifth floor apartment. She made herself a promise to get in better shape. She shouldn't be out of breath, even with the smoking. It was a week until her birthday, another year gone. This birthday was a milestone, for her, not for most people. Thirty-six, half her life lived before what her father had done, and half her life after. If you could call what she did living, perhaps it was just surviving.

The gig tonight had been great. The glow of appreciation from the audience still warmed her. It was two am, but maybe Rafe would still be awake, maybe the night didn't have to end. Maybe the void would be filled for a little while longer.

Sorting her apartment key to the top of the ring, she pushed open the stairwell door. The sight at the end of the hall, across from her own apartment, stopped her from taking the next step. Two men in overcoats and cheap suits stood staring through the open door of her neighbor's apartment. The stairwell door slammed behind her, and both men turned to stare.

Police. She reached behind her for the door, not sure why she felt the need to flee, but already thinking of where she'd go.

A uniformed cop stepped out of the apartment and whispered something to one of the men. The other took a step toward her. He held out his ID and she saw a shield on the card, one she didn't recognize. It didn't matter, they were obviously cops; she'd learned to recognize the attitude.

"Ma'am, this floor is closed."

Monique shook her head and stepped forward. No one was going to tell her she couldn't get into her home. She needed a shower, and a meal. "I live there," she said, pointing to her door. "What's going on?"

The detective – he must be a detective that kind of suit was almost a uniform for them – made a comment to his partner. Monique couldn't make out the words, but she figured it was something to do with making her go away. He turned back and said, "If you would like to answer a few questions, we can let you into your apartment."

He looked reasonable, and Monique didn't have anything to hide. She shoved away a little voice that told her to call a lawyer before talking to them, that the last time she'd talked to a detective it hadn't turned out well. "Sure, let's get this over with."

She tried not to look through the open door as she passed. She hated the kind of people who slowed down to look at accidents. She told herself that whatever was in there wouldn't be good. But her head turned almost as though someone had moved it for her. The uniformed cop pulled the door shut, but it was too late. She'd seen.

There was a lot of blood and a body. He, or maybe it, now that he was dead, was broken apart like someone had taken an ax and chopped him into two pieces at the waist.

Monique closed her eyes and slipped her key into the lock, feeling the presence of the cops behind her, reassuring now instead of threatening. She glanced at the mirror in the hall, needing to know what the cops were seeing. Her normally pale skin looked dull, reflecting the shock she felt from the scene across the hall, her green eyes shining from behind her messy bangs.

The shaking was already starting. She clenched her fist to keep the panic from taking over. It stopped the trembling but didn't wipe out the vision of all the blood. She could handle this. She'd handled worse. She had to keep it together. Swallowing the bile percolating in the back of her throat, Monique pointed to the stools at the kitchen counter and turned on the coffee pot. She held up two mugs in query, and both detectives nodded. "Okay, what do you want to ask?"

"Thanks," the first detective said. "I'm Detective Watson, Larry. This is my partner, Mike Adams." The other cop, younger than Watson, nodded. "Let's start with your name?"

She cleared her throat, hoping they didn't take it as a sign of weakness. "Monique Duchesne." She knew better than to volunteer any information. Anything she offered would be used as a thread to find questions that she wouldn't want to answer.

"And how long have you lived here?"

She noticed Adams write in the notebook while Watson asked the questions. "Five years." The coffee started dripping, so she went to get the milk from the fridge.

"Where do you come from?"

That was an odd question. "What do you mean?"

"You know, we all came here from somewhere. Where did your folks come from?"

"Why?"

Watson shrugged. "Just curious. Why don't you want to answer?"

There it was. Cops didn't like it when you held back information. Even if the question had nothing to do with whatever crime they were investigating. Monique was tempted to tell him to mind his own business, but she worried that he'd use that against her. "My dad emigrated from Yugoslavia. My mom was fourth generation Canadian."

He nodded, and Adams made a note. Watson continued. "And what do you do, Monique? For a living?"

Damn. The questions were going to come no matter what she did. "I sing at Blue Scene and I do a bit of tour guide stuff. Why do you need to know that?"

Mike Adams looked up from his notebook. "I thought I recognized you. You've got a great voice."

Monique smiled, but didn't let down her guard as she poured coffee. "Thanks. So why do you need to know about my work?"

Detective Watson ignored her question and sipped his coffee. "So is that where you were tonight?"

"Yes, I got there around nine and left about fifteen minutes before you saw me. Is this where I should tell you I want my lawyer?"

"No, the victim's been dead more than an hour. We got an anonymous call and when we got here... well, you saw what we saw. I'm sorry about that." He rubbed his forehead and Monique realized she wasn't the only one pretending to be unaffected by the horror across the hall.

Another sip and Watson asked, "Did you know him?"

She loosened her grip on the mug before she snapped the handle. The panic wouldn't push away, this needed to be over soon, or she'd collapse while they were in her home. She shook her head and rubbed at a spot on the counter. "He only moved in last month. I said hi to him once, and I think he had an accent, maybe eastern European. It was hard to tell from just a 'good morning'. The guy liked Death Metal and didn't understand you could play music at less than full volume."

"Did he have any visitors?" Watson was watching her closely.

Monique shook her head again and rose to put her mug in the sink. Leaning against the counter, she said, "I didn't pay much attention. I don't remember hearing anyone knock on his door." She crossed her arms, hoping they would get the hint that she wanted to be finished with the questions.

The detectives rose leaving their half-empty coffee mugs on the table. "Thanks. I guess if there's anything else we need, we can reach you here?"

"Here or the club. Should I be worried about someone breaking in?"

Detective Adams slid his notebook into his pocket, retrieving a business card. "Make sure you lock your door, and don't open it to strangers. If you need anything, or something happens, call."

Monique took the card; a list of contact numbers filled the back. "So, it wasn't random?"

Detective Watson looked her up and down. Monique felt the dismissal in his glance. "We don't discuss open cases with the public. Just be careful, and you should be okay."

She kept her eyes on the floor as she let the two detectives out. Locking the door and shoving a chair under the handle to block any forced entry didn't make her feel any safer. She slid to the floor and gave up fighting the inevitable. The darkness crawled over her as she curled into a ball, trembling with the memory of the room across the hall.

MONIQUE UNTANGLED herself from the sheets and stretched the last vestiges of sleep from her body. She could hear Rafe in the kitchen. Judging by the fingers of light pushing through the slats of the blinds, it was lunchtime. She stumbled to the bathroom to brush her teeth and try to deal with the mess sleep had made of her hair.

She'd called Rafe an hour after the cops left. He'd buzzed her into the building and waited at the elevator. His warmth and strength driving the last of the fear from her.

Ten minutes after leaving Rafe's bed, she snuck into the kitchen to wrap her arms around him. He made her feel safe, at least until she remembered that safety was just a temporary feeling. Her neighbor had probably felt safe. Her mother had too.

She pulled a mug from the cupboard and poured herself coffee. Rafe hated her smoking in his apartment, so she'd have to wait for her other vice.

"Afternoon, babe. You hungry?"

She watched him flip a grilled cheese sandwich in the pan. His strong hands holding the spatula delicately. His dark skin was as different from her pallor as everything else about him was. He glowed with health, and he carried a comfortable amount of padding on his frame. She was thin enough to garner looks of concern from strangers.

"You know I am."

He flipped the sandwich onto a plate and reached for the bread to start another. "Are you ready to tell me what exactly happened last night?"

Monique shrugged. When she'd called Rafe, she'd told him there was trouble with a neighbor. Leaving out the details meant she didn't have to argue with him about how unsafe her building was.

"What makes you think there's anything else to tell?" Monique added a pile of potato chips from the bag on the counter to her plate.

"Nightmares. You were fighting something all night." His attention was focused on the contents of the pan. "You'll feel better if you tell me what happened." He glanced at her. "You know I hate that you live there, so I won't mention it again."

"I like that building, and I can afford the rent." She also

liked her independence and knew Rafe wanted her to move into his place. Monique wasn't ready for that, maybe never would be. It was an old argument and she didn't want to have it again. "Sorry."

"I said I wouldn't talk about it and I won't. But unless you plan to work this out in your sleep, you need to tell someone how you feel." He muttered something else to the pan as he flipped his own sandwich.

"I don't need to –"

He slapped the spatula on the counter. "You do. You keep saying you don't need to talk about your feelings, but you're human and that means you feel something. It will turn you sour, Monique. If you don't deal with this, it will dry you up and kill you."

Monique felt the familiar tightening of her stomach at the memory of the last time she'd talked about her feelings. But she didn't want to lose sleep, so maybe Rafe was right, talking about it would make it go away faster. "Okay. Look my neighbor got murdered last night. I'm fine. I didn't even know him." Rafe didn't know what it took to talk to a psychologist. How they twisted everything you told them.

"Did you see what they did to him?" Rafe dropped his plate onto the table. "If you did, it would explain your nightmares."

"What do you mean, what they did to him?" There was no hope of getting out of this without a fight if Rafe had any of the details.

"I knew something happened. I checked the police radio transmissions. And then I called my friend in the morgue. He told me what the body looked like when it came in." Rafe had friends all over the city in all kinds of professions. His work as an investigative blogger meant he needed contacts. The goriest stories brought the most hits to his blog, and that meant more affiliate money. Monique didn't like the fact that he'd used those contacts on her. That he'd known what happened before she decided to tell him, like he was testing her.

No longer hungry, Monique pushed her plate away. Her hands reaching for the pack of cigarettes in her purse before remembering Rafe had no ashtrays. "Okay. Yes I did see it. Yes, it was horrible, but I am fine. I didn't know the guy. From what the cops said, it was personal, so I'm fine. I'm fine." She hated the shake in her voice at the end.

Rafe pushed her plate back toward her. "Eat before you get so thin you disappear. If you were okay, why did you call me? If you are okay, why did you have nightmares?"

"I called you because I didn't want to spend the night alone. I was already going to call you before I saw the... and I don't know why I had nightmares." She took a bite of the sandwich hoping she could get it down her tightening throat. At least it would give her some time to cool off before she ended up saying something that would hurt him. That's what always happened.

"You say that all the time. Nothing bothers you apparently."

Monique didn't want to have this argument, not now and, preferably, not ever. "I just don't see the point of talking about feeling crappy. I really don't feel that bad about it. Is that wrong? You used to like the fact that I didn't weep over stupid things." And it was safer not to care too much.

Rafe sighed, and she could see him work to hold in his temper. "Sometimes I feel like I'm the only one who feels anything in this relationship." He looked away from her. "If it's just about the sex, let me know."

"It's not." She stood and went to the living area of the open plan apartment. "I'm going home. I think it's best if we don't talk for a couple of days." If he really loved her, he'd let it go. Maybe a few days apart would cool everything down again. She started for the door.

"Are you going to call me? Or is this your way of ending it? I deserve better than this if it is." His voice was quiet, and Monique knew she'd hurt him more than she'd intended.

"I'll call you," she said as she left.

Waiting for the elevator, she wondered if he was right. Was this relationship all about the sex? Why did he have to want more than she could give? He knew why she couldn't give him more, and it had been enough until recently.

Perhaps it was time to end it, before he got hurt. Perhaps she should take advantage of this fight to leave.

When the elevator arrived, Monique pulled out her cigarettes, ready to light up as soon as she stepped out of the front door of his building. Nicotine helped fill that hole inside where other people probably kept the feelings she hadn't felt since her eighteenth birthday.

CHAPTER 2

Later, Monique turned away from her window. Staring at the rain wasn't going to get her anywhere. If Rafe wanted to break up, so be it. She would survive. She always survived. She slipped her iPod into the speaker dock and let it run through her favorite playlist. Music always helped no matter what mood she was in or how bad the day had been. Nerves were making her jumpy. She needed to do something. The weak light through the window didn't show it, but her home needed a cleaning. Anything that would help take her mind off the memory of the blood across the hall.

It didn't take long, but the familiar steps of dusting, polishing, and scouring brought a measure of peace. The staleness that dulled her senses lifted, replaced with the clean sharp smell of lemon and bleach. Monique threw the cleaning cloths into the laundry basket then leaned out through the open window and lit a cigarette, inhaling deeply. The rain had stopped while she was cleaning, the clouds evaporating to reveal the sky, pale blue just waiting for the sun to set and display stars.

She knew logically that the argument with Rafe wasn't going to end the relationship. In her head, the reality of his accusation rang true, and she couldn't argue against anything he'd said. In her heart, something twisted the words into weapons and truth didn't matter. It wasn't her fault she couldn't feel anything. He knew her history, and he knew what she'd overcome. She hated that he was trying to change her. She knew she was broken. She didn't need anyone to fix her.

Broken had worked for the last eighteen years.

She shook her head and stubbed the cigarette into the ashtray she held. Thinking wouldn't solve the problem. She needed to talk to Rafe, but she also needed to take some time to get over the fight first. If she called him right now, there was a real chance she'd make things worse while trying to fix them.

In the kitchen, Monique started a pot of coffee and then picked up the material Walk in The Past had sent about the new ghost walk she was leading in a couple of days. Vancouver had enough history to make hundreds of different tours, and she filled some time with leading tourists through the more seedy parts of town. The stories she told about the history of the area seemed to entertain. Some of them were true, and some complete fiction.

Halfway through the material, Monique heard a door slam across the hall. Fear shot through her entire body. Were the police back? She walked to the peephole and glanced out, but there was nothing to see. Monique leaned against the door. The noise had definitely come from across the hall. Wanting to avoid going back to picking over her relationship defects, and bored with the reading material, she turned the lock quietly and darted across the hall.

Monique tried to look through the peephole into the apartment, but the distortion blurred all the details. She leaned against the door, careful not to break the crime tape, and listened. Yes, there was something going on in there. Someone was tossing heavy things around.

She pushed away from the door and ducked back into her own apartment. Should she call the police? What if it was something innocent? She reached for the phone to call Rafe for advice before she remembered the fight.

She put her eye to her own peephole, but there was no one in the hall. She knew that calling the cops was the right thing to do. She knew it wasn't something innocent. Why would someone innocently be going through the murdered guy's apartment? She glanced at the phone and made her decision.

"Hey, cut it out," a woman shrieked.

Monique ran back to the door to see who had come from the apartment. It wasn't a stranger. Mac, the guy who lived next door stood in her line of sight. He had his arm around a skinny blond chick, a bottle of Jack in the hand dangling near her breasts. He slobbered a kiss on her cheek and then elbowed his door open. They fell through it, both giggling.

Glancing at the apartment across from her, Monique decided to wait. If she called the cops now, she didn't have any details. If she kept watch, maybe she would see something useful. She hated her father for many things, but mostly right now, because he'd made her afraid of the police, and that was making her look for excuses to delay the call.

Monique took the phone from its cradle and held it ready to call if something happened.

Keeping her eye to the peephole, she couldn't help imagining what was going on in the apartment. Why would someone need to come back there? Had they used a key? She tried to think back over the month since the guy had moved in. Alexi, that was his name. She'd told the police she hadn't noticed any visitors, was that really the case? There was that one time, some older guy was banging on Alexi's door. But he wasn't home, so that probably doesn't count.

Music started thumping out of Mac's apartment. It sounded

like a porn soundtrack. Monique snorted a laugh. At least someone was having fun.

She checked the clock. Whoever was in the apartment had been there for fifteen minutes. They might not come out for a while. If she'd phoned the cops when she first heard the door, they would be here by now. She pressed 911 and waited for the response. Her hand trembled. She shook it out to release the tension, hoping that it would work, and that the trembling wasn't the start of a panic attack.

"911 what is your emergency?"

"I... um, I saw someone go into an apartment," she said. Damn nerves, damn history.

"Ma'am?"

Monique took a breath. "Sorry. I live across from the guy who got murdered... at the Montrose... on 15th... near Main. Someone is in the apartment."

"The police are on their way. Are you in danger?"

Keeping her eye on the door across the way, Monique said, "No. Whoever it is doesn't know I heard anything. They are still in there. I heard them tossing stuff around."

"The police will be there in two minutes. I'll stay on the line with you until they arrive."

"No, I'm fine. I'll wait for them. Thanks." Monique hung up the phone and put it back on the cradle.

A sound drew her back to the peephole. A man, tall, skinny, and bald was locking the door behind him. He turned to Mac's door and said something Monique couldn't make out, but he followed it with a dirty leer.

Then he turned to stare at her apartment.

She jumped back at the sight of his dark eyes burning through the door. He looked like something from a horror movie. The one monster that looked human until you got close and saw the blankness behind his eyes.

Telling herself he couldn't see her, Monique put her eye back to the peephole and was relieved that his gaze was on the floor. She watched him bend and retrieve a black gym bag from the carpet. He checked the weight of the bag and then headed to the stairwell.

The elevator chimed just as she heard the stairwell door bang shut. Monique pulled open her door to see detectives Watson and Adams step into the hall.

"He went down the stairs," she kept her voice quiet, not wanting the man to know she'd seen anything. "He just went down."

The two detectives ripped open the door and raced though. "Stop! Police!"

Monique heard the words then a clatter of feet on the uncarpeted stairs. Glancing at Mac's door in case the sound had penetrated the bump kachunk of the music, Monique retreated to her apartment. If the cops were successful, she was done for the day. That would be fine. She didn't need to get involved. She could get back to her life.

Monique grabbed a bottle of Malbec from the rack and unscrewed the top. After pouring a glass, she opened all the windows and lit a cigarette. To hell with the smell. Wine glass in hand, she stood inside the living room watching the street, hoping to see the arrest. Nothing but a few pedestrians and some guy trying to park a jeep in a space big enough for a Smart car.

She stubbed out the cigarette and blew the last lungful of smoke through the open window.

Maybe it happened out in the alley. She knew the cops didn't need to let her know what happened, but it would be nice. The memory of those black eyes burning through the peephole made her skin crawl. There was no way he would know she was there. It was just a coincidence.

She reached for her cellphone. Maybe calling Rafe would help her settle. As her fingers traced the pattern to unlock it, she decided to wait. Phoning Rafe only when she was struggling seemed unfair. If she wasn't ready to commit to him, she shouldn't be ready to use him.

In the kitchen, she topped off the wine and reached for a package of Ramen noodles. Then dropped them as someone banged on her door, and the shock stopped her heart. She braced herself on the counter to stop the sudden rush of dizziness that flooded her when her heart started again, pounding so hard it felt like she was jerking to a four-part beat.

"Hang on," she called, taking one last deep breath before she swallowed a gulp of wine.

"Ms. Duchesne?" It was Watson and he sounded worried.

If they were here, the guy must have gotten away. "Yes, just a second." She checked through the peephole before opening the door, just in case.

"Are you okay?" Detective Adams asked.

Monique recognized the canned emotions, meant to put a suspect, or victim, at ease. The good cop part of the equation. She knew to avoid believing he really cared. "I'm fine. He didn't see me. I swear I didn't confront him. Just tell me what happened. Is he still out there?"

"I can't tell you much," Watson said, glancing at the coffee pot.

Monique wasn't planning to make them feel at home, so she ignored his hint. "Does that mean you didn't catch him?"

Adams pulled out his notebook and waited for Watson to take the lead.

"We missed him. He could have hidden too many places when he went out the back. We need to know exactly what happened. Start with what you saw."

Taking a sip of her wine, Monique sat on one of the stools at the counter. "I heard a noise.... the door slamming across the hall. I wasn't sure what was going on, so I listened at the door and heard someone banging around inside."

Watson leaned against the counter and crossed his arms. "Why didn't you call us then?"

"How do you know I didn't?"

"Did you? Was he only in there a minute or two?"

Monique couldn't think of a way to avoid the question, so she shrugged. "I wasn't sure that there was any problem. It could have been you guys. I would have looked pretty stupid calling the cops if it was you."

He twisted his lips then relaxed as though he'd made a decision. "No you wouldn't. What you did was stupid. If it happens again, call. So you want to give your statement here, in your apartment?"

Wary of the change in his attitude, Monique said, "Here is fine. Like I said, I heard someone banging around the apartment. Then I decided to call. I don't know maybe I realized cops would have removed the crime tape, or something."

Adams was scribbling notes. "What did you see?"

"When I was on the phone the guy came out. Maybe fifty, around six foot, maybe a couple of hundred pounds... No, he was really thin, probably more like one-eighty. Shaved head, gray stubble. Am I going too fast?"

Adams looked up. "No, carry on."

"Okay. Weird eyes. Black like they were all pupil. Oh, maybe he was high."

"Any distinguishing marks? Scars? Tattoos?"

Monique closed her eyes and reluctantly drew on the memory of that face. "No. Just the eyes were weird."

"Anything else?"

She ran the memory like a movie. "He had a black gym bag.

It seemed heavy, but there was no sound when he lifted it, so whatever was inside it wasn't hard, or metal."

Watson straightened. "Have you ever seen him before?"

Monique shook her head. Then memory flashed. "Wait. There was a tattoo on his hand, the back of his hand. It was faded but I think it was an eagle... it was clutching something square." She held out her hand for the notebook. "Let me draw it for you." She sketched quickly. An eagle's head in profile, but she couldn't put any detail around the square. She pushed it back to Adams.

"Anything else?" Watson asked.

"No that's it. So, you can go now." The words felt harsh, but Monique wanted them out of her house, wanted to start putting this behind her. She'd had plenty of practice at that.

"Do you have somewhere else to stay?" Watson actually looked like he cared. She reminded herself he was just playing good cop.

"I'm fine here." Monique hoped she was right, but what if the guy came back? "He doesn't know I called you." If he came looking, there were only six apartments on the floor. It wouldn't take him long to figure out who did call. "It could have been someone downstairs, or anyone who saw him come into the building. Anyway, what are you going to do?"

"We'll send a team to check out the apartment. They'll remove the tape like you thought, so you don't think there's a problem. Then we'll get back to the investigation." Watson gestured to Adams. "We have to go. Be careful, Ms. Duchesne."

Monique strode to the door and pulled it open. "I'm a big girl. I won't open my door to strangers. Just catch the guy, and we'll all be fine."

"It's on the list of cases. We'll solve it, just be careful."

She watched them check the lock on the door across the hall and then leave. When the elevator closed, Monique stepped back into her apartment and locked herself in. Pulling a chair away from the dining table, she jammed it under the handle again.

What did he mean? It's on the list of cases? How many of these kinds of brutal murders did they have on the list? What did it take for a case to get priority?

How long did she need to keep the door locked?

MORE DRAMA, more thrills. Use the QR code to get your copy of the next City Crimes books, THE DRAGON AT THE EDGE OF THE MAP

FREE EBOOK

Claim your copy of Buying Into Death when you sign up for my newsletter and follow Charity as she solves her fastest case yet!

ALSO BY P A WILSON

For more books by P A Wilson

Use the QR code below or go to pawilson.ca

ABOUT THE AUTHOR

Perry Wilson is a Canadian author based in Vancouver, BC who has big ideas and an itch to tell stories. Having spent some time on university, a career, and life in general, she returned to writing in 2008 and hasn't looked back since (well, maybe a little, but only while parallel parking).

She is a member of the Vancouver Writers Social Group, The Royal City Literary Arts Society, and The Surrey Writing Workshop. Perry has self-published several novels. She writes the Madeline Journeys, a fantasy series about a high-powered lawyer who finds herself trapped in a magical world, the Quinn Larson Quests, which follows the adventures of a wizard named Quinn who must contend with volatile fae in the heart of Vancouver, and the Charity Deacon Investigations, a mystery thriller series about a private eye who tends to fall into serious trouble with her cases, and The Riverton Romances, a series based in a small town in Oregon, one of her favorite states. Her stand-alone novels are Breaking the Bonds, Closing the Circle, and The Dragon at The Edge of The Map.

For more information
www.pawilson.ca
pawilson@pawilson.ca

f X

ACKNOWLEDGMENTS

People think that the process of writing is solitary. That's not the case for me. I have help from so many people it would be hard to acknowledge everyone, but I'll give it a try.

The support and inspiration I get from my writer's groups is incalculable. The Vancouver Writers Social Group opens my mind to other ways of telling a story. The Royal City Literary Arts Society gives me the opportunity to meet and share with other writers who have more knowledge than I do. The Other 11 Months group is where I learn about getting the words on the page. And my critique group who helps me find the best parts of the story I want to tell. Thanks to all of the members of these great groups.

Last of all, but definitely a huge part of the process, my beta readers. These are the people who love stories and are willing, and more than able, to tell me if my finished story is ready for you, my readers.